HELL! SAID THE

Michael Arlen was born Dikran Kouyoumdjian in Bulgaria in 1895 to an Armenian merchant family. In 1901, his family moved to England, where Arlen went on to attend school at Malvern College. He enrolled as a medical student at the University of Edinburgh but did not stay long, deciding instead to move to London and make a living by writing. His earliest magazine contributions were under his birth name, but with the publication of his first book, *London Venture* (1920), he adopted the pen name of Michael Arlen, and in 1922 when he was naturalized as a British subject, he legally changed his name to Michael Arlen.

Arlen's first books enjoyed some success, but his 1924 novel *The Green Hat* was a runaway worldwide bestseller. The novel was adapted for the stage on Broadway and in London's West End and was the basis for a silent Hollywood film starring Greta Garbo. *The Green Hat* made Arlen rich and famous almost overnight, and he became an international celebrity.

In 1927, Arlen, feeling ill, joined D. H. Lawrence in Florence, where the latter was working on *Lady Chatterley's Lover*, in which Arlen would later find himself portrayed as Michaelis. The following year, Arlen married Countess Atalanta Mercati in Cannes; they had a son and a daughter.

Arlen continued to write during the remainder of the 1920s and 1930s, but none of his works met with the same success as *The Green Hat*. When Arlen found his loyalty to England questioned during World War II, he and his family moved to New York, where during the last ten years of his life he suffered from writer's block. He died of cancer in 1956.

Mark Valentine is the author of several collections of short fiction and has published biographies of Arthur Machen and Sarban. He is the editor of *Wormwood*, a journal of the literature of the fantastic, supernatural, and decadent, and has previously written the introductions to editions of Walter de la Mare, Robert Louis Stevenson, L. P. Hartley, and others, and has introduced John Davidson's *Earl Lavender* (1895), R. C. Ashby's *He Arrived at Dusk* (1933), Claude Houghton's *This Was Ivor Trent* (1935), and Oliver Onions's *The Hand of Kornelius Voyt* (1939) for Valancourt Books.

Cover: Because no example of the original dust jacket in a condition suitable for reproduction could be located, the cover of this edition is a recreation by M.S. Corley that replicates the design of the first U.S. edition, published by Doubleday in 1934.

By Michael Arlen

The London Venture (1920)

The Romantic Lady (1921)

"Piracy" (1922)

These Charming People (1923)

The Green Hat (1924)

May Fair (1925)

Ghost Stories (1927)

Young Men in Love (1927)

Lily Christine (1928)

Babes in the Wood (1929)

Men Dislike Women (1931)

Man's Mortality (1933)

Hell! said the Duchess (1934)

The Crooked Coronet (1937)

The Flying Dutchman (1939)

HELL! SAID THE DUCHESS

A Bed-Time Story

by

MICHAEL ARLEN

With a new introduction by

MARK VALENTINE

VALANCOURT BOOKS
Richmond, Virginia
2013

Hell! said the Duchess by Michael Arlen
First published London: Heinemann, 1934
First Valancourt Books edition 2013

Published by Valancourt Books, Richmond, Virginia
Publisher & Editor: James D. Jenkins
20th Century Series Editor: Simon Stern, University of Toronto
http://www.valancourtbooks.com

Library of Congress Cataloging-in-Publication Data
Arlen, Michael, 1895-1956.
Hell! said the Duchess : a bed-time story / by Michael Arlen ; with a new introduction by Mark Valentine.—First Valancourt Books edition.
pages ; cm.—(20th century series)
ISBN 978-1-939140-52-4 (alk. pbk.)
1. Murder–Investigation–Fiction. 2. London (England)–Fiction. I. Title.
PR6001.R7H45 2013
823'.912–dc23
2013017951

All Valancourt Books publications are printed on acid free paper that meets all ANSI standards for archival quality paper.

Cover by M. S. Corley
Set in Dante MT 12/15

INTRODUCTION

The period just after the First World War and before the Depression of the Thirties has passed into legend as a time of wild abandon and fateful devil-may-care: these were the doomed days of the Bright Young Things. F. Scott Fitzgerald was the American chronicler of those years, but in Britain it was Michael Arlen who most caught the Twenties mood, and especially in his suave supernatural thriller of 1934, *Hell! said the Duchess*.

In this and a few other dashing and cynical books, which the *New Statesman* typified as unequalled in evoking the *"dandysme* of the soul," Arlen wrote of the fast set of Mayfair and Belgravia, those who were to be termed the Lost Generation. His characters are jaded young war heroes still hungering for excitement; newly emboldened and abandoned heroines; raffish cads and outcasts from convention; or, as in this book, beautiful but strange aristocrats. The appeal of Arlen's insouciant characters was so great that he became one of the first million-sellers and revelled in fame and luxury. He was one of the first media celebrities, whose every move was newsworthy. Yet he wanted to be taken seriously as a writer, was proud of his friendships with D. H. Lawrence, Somerset Maugham, Ernest Hemingway, and other literary figures, and in his last years despaired at his inability to write something new.

Today, Michael Arlen remains little more than a footnote in histories of 20th century fiction. Perhaps this is partly because of his obscure background. He was born on 16 November 1895 in Rustchuk, Bulgaria, to an Armenian merchant family fleeing persecution. They came to England in 1901 and settled in Lancashire. Christened as Dikran Kouyoumdjian, Arlen attended an English public school ("So I'm completely self-educated," he quipped), and, briefly, Edinburgh University. Breaking away from his family, who disowned him, he went to London to put into practice his firm belief that writing was his vocation.

As a foreigner, he was not permitted to play any part in the war effort and so lived frugally, scraping a living from newspaper and magazine contributions. He created a poetic, consumptive alter ego, Michael Arlen, and when his writing began to attract attention, adopted the name for himself. He became a naturalized British subject in 1922, and took the pen-name as his legal name too. Armenian refugees had been the object of pity in Britain, but Arlen knew that this pity was mixed with liberal doses of condescension which a proud race found hard to bear. He saw he would never be fully accepted in his adopted country, and his success certainly bred resentment. Another popular author, Sydney Horler, sneeringly described him as "the only Armenian who never tried to sell me a carpet."

So Arlen set himself to become more English than the most aristocratic of the English. Even when he was struggling in the early years, his tailoring was always impeccable, he perfected the languid air of the born dilettante and beguiled the opposite sex with his studied, immaculate manners. But he also played upon his foreignness, describing himself as "every other inch a gentleman" and "a case of pernicious Armenia."

His first book, *The London Venture* (1920), was a lightly fictionalized account of his early literary struggles. On its appearance, it was thought by some to be a pseudonymous work by George Moore, whose candid memoirs written in an ornamental, Eighteen Nineties style were highly acclaimed. Full of literary references, the book is notable for its championing of D. H. Lawrence, whom Arlen had befriended when they were both beginning their writing careers. It was Lawrence who advised Arlen that he would be best advised to write fantasy, because of his Romantic notions. Later, much of Arlen is to be seen in Lady Chatterley's *first* lover, in Lawrence's notorious novel (1928), where he is scarcely disguised as Michaelis, a successful society playwright: "Connie really wondered at this queer, melancholy specimen of extraordinary success . . . Sometimes he was handsome: sometimes, as he looked sideways, downwards, and the light fell on him, he had the silent, enduring beauty of a carved ivory Negro mask, with his rather full eyes, and the strong queerly-arched brows, the immobile, compressed mouth . . . Connie felt a sudden, strange leap of sympathy for him, a leap mingled with compassion, and tinged with repulsion . . . The outsider! The outsider! And they called him a bounder!"

His first major success was *"Piracy"* (1922; the title includes the inverted commas), which recounted the life of Ivor Pelham Marley in a decade spanning the war years. A writer of romances, from an aristocratic background ("Missed an earldom by an heir's breath" says one character), Marley epitomized the sense of futility of the war generation. He has a doomed love for provocative and glamorous Virginia Tarlyon, a Soho bohemian as well as a Society figure: "Virginia has a mind like a cathedral," proclaims her father. "Of course every cathedral has its gargoyles," he adds wistfully. Her appearance—slim, white-faced like a carnival mask, delicate—and her lifestyle were based on the poet and heiress Nancy Cunard, whom Arlen had met in 1920. At one point, Aldous Huxley regarded Arlen as a rival for Nancy's allegiance, and he satirizes him in his novel *Those Barren Leaves* (1925), where he is travestied as "the swarthy Syrian with the blue jowl and the silver monocle . . . he never lost an opportunity of telling people he was a poet; he was for ever discussing the inconveniences and compensating advantages of possessing an artistic temperament." Though Huxley altered Arlen's race and physical appearance, the urgent insistence on his writing was pure Arlen.

"Piracy" was a great success, for it portrayed both the unconventional, spontaneous, consciously modern life of those artistic circles which gathered in the Café Royal and the Eiffel Tower Restaurant in Soho, and certain ageless qualities of gallantry and chivalry which were seen to be bound to fall under the onslaught of mass movements and mass industry. The novel's theme may perhaps be summed up in the defiant toast offered by the last gentleman in England in a fantasy scene conjured by Marley in which the old order is besieged by armies of the *nouveaux riches*: "For King and Cocktails!" he proclaims.

The novel was followed by Arlen's most successful collection of linked short stories, *These Charming People* (1923), with its splendid subtitle, *"Being a Tapestry of the Fortunes, Follies, Adventures, Gallantries and General Activities of Shelmerdene (that lovely lady), Lord Tarlyon, Mr. Michael Wagstaffe, Mr. Ralph Wyndham Trevor and Some Others of their Friends of the Lighter Sort."* The fifteen stories are quicker in wit and cleverer in storyline than his earlier work and their twist endings and elegant, sardonic style suggest a strange hybrid of the American short story master O. Henry and the epigrammatic, quintessentially English Saki (H. H. Munro). For the first time, Arlen introduces fantasy and the macabre to his tales, and we find the tone of dark insouciance he was later to perfect in *Hell! said the Duchess*. The bizarre adventures his characters find in the London streets suggest the influence of Robert Louis Stevenson's *New Arabian Nights*. All the tales are laced with fine irony and understatement, and a kind of bantering tone with the reader which was becoming Arlen's hallmark.

But it was *The Green Hat* (1924) that precipitated Arlen into a world of unimagined acclaim and prosperity. The novel was quite simply the novel of the year, seized upon as the poetically true testament to a brilliant, daring and doomed generation. The owner of the green hat is Iris Storm, whose wild pursuit of pleasure in the parties, masquerades, night clubs and restaurants of London and Paris has led to her reputation as a "shameless, shameful" woman: but paradoxically there is some calm reserve in her which seems to imply a secret inner grace. The melodramatic narrative, written in what one critic called an "opium dream style," sonorous with exotic and cosmic images, may only draw a wry smile today.

Enriched by the success of the book, Arlen made his home on the French Riviera where he could indulge his taste for the high life in full. He mingled with minor royalty and international aristocracy, and married the Greek countess Atalanta Mercati. Yet he remained mindful of his origins in a persecuted people: the story goes that when he saw Goebbels strutting on a hotel balcony below his room, he carefully prepared a Martini and poured it languidly over the Nazi minister's head.

The Green Hat was clearly going to be difficult to follow, and

Arlen bought time by publishing next a further collection of stories featuring the "charming people" circle, *May Fair* (1925). In the epilogue, "Farewell, These Charming People," Satan attends a brilliant, world-weary dinner party: "'Young man,' said the Lord Chancellor severely, 'are you seriously implying that you are the Prince of Darkness?' 'We do not recognize that title,' cried Lady Surplice. 'It is not in Burke, Debrett, or the Almanach de Gotha—.'" Stories in which a decaying aristocracy become mingled with the sinister or supernatural are frequent in Gothic fiction— such as Bram Stoker's Count Dracula and M.P. Shiel's Prince Zaleski. But Michael Arlen introduced a more modish, scintillant, mocking tone to this Gothic motif, fully exemplified by *Hell! said the Duchess*, his most overt work in the form.

It was, of course, another *Green Hat* the public wanted, and Arlen had three attempts to oblige them, with *Young Men in Love* (1927), *Lily Christine* (1928) and *Men Dislike Women* (1931). On the strength of his name, these all sold well, but none received anything like the adulation of *The Green Hat*. The first, ominously, includes a portrait of a fantastically popular author who finds he has "had enough of publicity," is "tired of making a fool of himself" and wants to be "a serious man, one of the world's workers." The author is taken to task for failing to write about "lords and champagne and lovely painted ladies": readers find him "very disappointing," publishers accuse him of ingratitude, and critics say he is "insincere" and "affected."

It is to Arlen's credit that he did not simply resign himself to the comfortable production of formula fiction, perennially fashioning a new form of Iris Storm to gratify the *Green Hat* fanatics: but his downfall was that he could not quite throw off his creation. He tried to break new ground with a serious futuristic novel, *Man's Mortality* (1933). This is set in the 1980s, when an international aircraft syndicate has monopolized all forms of global communications and effectively controls the world. There has been peace and a measure of progress for fifty years, but now a generation of younger officers in the service are reviving ideas of freedom and national identity. Arlen tries to explore the tension between these ideals and the need for stability, while still giving his readers the action and adventure of a thriller, but the result is unconvincing. Though he was proud of this attempt to tackle profounder themes, Arlen's novel was indifferently received, most critics comparing it unfavourably to Aldous Huxley's *Brave New World*, which had appeared the year before.

But if there is one book from his later period that does deserve more attention it is the strikingly entitled *Hell! said the Duchess*. Here, Arlen catches some of the contemporary turmoil of the Thirties, with the unemployment marches, Fascist and Communist demonstrations, social upheaval and a ponderous, stagnant National Government. But this forms the background to a bizarre thriller about a series of "Jane the Ripper" murders perpetrated by a young, unknown feminine killer on working class men. The beautiful Duchess of Dove is suspected, but Scotland Yard cannot bring themselves to believe that an aristocrat could be responsible, especially in view of the sexual nature of the crimes. As agitation to arrest the irreproachable Duchess increases, a private detective begins to find discrepancies in the case against her. In a strong and rather daring climax to the novel, we learn what lies behind the mystery of the Duchess's apparent complicity in the crimes. Suffice to say there are echoes of Robert Louis Stevenson's *Strange Case of Dr Jekyll and Mr Hyde* and Arthur Machen's *The Great God Pan*. But Arlen has made a macabre romance for the modern age.

Hell! said the Duchess was Arlen's last great success. He returned even more closely to his original formula with his next book, a collection of short stories (or "legends" as he called them) entitled *The Crooked Coronet* (1937), dedicated to a princess of the deposed royal house of Serbia, whom Arlen knew from his South of France circle. The eleven stories include two new adventures of the Cavalier of the Streets and a return for some of the "charming people" of his earlier volumes. But there are signs of repetition in the plots and the witticisms of these stories and the preposterousness of incident is more forced, as if even Arlen was tiring of his own inventiveness. The one unusual tale is the legend of "The Black

Archangel," in which a winged West African messiah leads an uprising against colonial rule. Despite the typically outré theme, the lead character is portrayed with some sympathy.

The Flying Dutchman (1939), Arlen's last new book, was another attempt to find a new direction. A political thriller, it is interesting today as a record of the troubled atmosphere of the years immediately before the Second World War. Ranging widely across the world, it links together revolutions, assassinations, riots and civil wars in a biting portrayal of humanity going out of control and moving remorselessly towards all-out war. After much intrigue and mystery, the novel unveils a nihilistic conspiracy, the Société de C, whose members are all outcasts from other extreme organizations, and whose sole aim is to act as agents provocateurs in every volatile situation they can find: but all is not quite what it seems. Once again, however, Arlen was to be disappointed by the response to his search for more challenging writing. The book was even less well received than *Man's Mortality*.

After he had ceased writing, Arlen's last years were tragic and wasted. He returned to England to serve as an air raid warden during the Second World War, but found the old suspicions of his foreign ancestry were stirred up again and left for America. He co-wrote a screenplay for a mild romantic comedy, *The Heavenly Body*, starring Hedy Lamarr, and found other Hollywood work. He created a TV detective, Gay Falcon, who was mildly popular for a short while. He was used to introduce a TV series of strange tales, and he recycled some old ideas to sell stories to American magazines. But his inspiration had gone, his flair for clever turns of phrase and unusual plots had faded. His son, Michael J. Arlen, has written a moving memoir of this time (*Exiles*, 1971) which portrays the aimlessness of his father's life, leisured but barren, a constant round of socializing with people who hardly knew him but were attracted by the old cachet of his name. He recalls too Arlen's long, lonely night-time pacings in their library, which would end as they began: with the white writing-paper on the desk still neatly stacked and unmarked. Michael Arlen died of cancer in New York on 23 June 1956.

Since then, Arlen's work has remained largely unregarded. *The Green Hat* has had periodic revivals as a touchstone novel for the Twenties, and a few of his macabre stories have been anthologized. But his glinting wit and literary bravado deserve a revival. *Hell! said the Duchess*, heady and lurid as a nightclub cocktail, swift and sleek as a Hispano-Suiza, is a wonderfully outré Art Deco fantasy that surely ought to lure a discerning new set of readers.

MARK VALENTINE

April 14, 2013

HELL! SAID THE DUCHESS

This book is inscribed
affectionately
by his friend and obedient servant
the author
to Valentine Browne
commonly known as Viscount Castlerosse
of London and Killarney
soldier, dandy, banker, gossip, golfer, philosopher
and
a man of good will

CHAPTER ONE

WHEN the writer permits himself the familiarity of calling her Mary Dove it is not from any disrespect to a lady of rank, nor with any pretensions to the intimate condescension of a lady of fashion. It is written so merely because he finds it a pleasant thing to set down the name: Mary Dove.

Now when the familiar history of our times comes to be written it will be the more readable for the inclusion of this quiet and gracious lady. Since she was so very quiet and lived so privately, it was by repute that her generation was enamoured of her, and there never was a person who was better spoken of in all the counties of England.

But it would be doing the lady an injustice to say merely that her loveliness was a treasured ornament of English life, both of the town and in the country, and it must be emphasised that she was admired not only for her slender beauty. For she was gifted with qualities of the mind and heart which endeared her to young and old alike, and her kindness was incorruptible by any prejudice whatsoever.

Thus she was much loved by all who knew her. While even the spiteful, who are always with us, could not but acknowledge that the Duchess of Dove would have been a knock-out in any station of life.

That is why the story of the misfortunes that beset her, unspeakably horrible though they were, must serve to adorn her reputation and exalt her memory.

John Charles Almeric Wingless St. Cloud Bull, 3rd Duke of Dove and Oldham, 4th Marquess of Rockneil, 9th Earl of Locroy, 4th Viscount Aberlaw, and 22nd Baron Pest of Cheadle, ensign in His Majesty's Brigade of Guards, was killed in a motor accident eight months after his marriage. The poor lad's death was made the more tragic by its indirect cause. He was on King's Guard within the ancient pile of St. James's Palace, and enjoying one of the excellent dinners provided for officers engaged on that august duty, when he was warned by telephone that his wife was enduring the agonies of premature labour pains. It was no doubt from driving altogether too fast through the tempting darkness of the Great North Road towards Dove Park that he collided with a lorry not far from Kettering and was instantly killed. He need not have hurried so. Or, had he been instructed in the pleasures of reading, he could have taken the train. For the yearly increase in motoring fatalities can be due to nothing so much as a distaste for reading, for which a railway carriage, whether made of wood or of steel, provides ample facilities. Indigestion had caused the young Duke's alarm, and the stricken young widow was delivered of a healthy son at the due time.

That was eleven years before the Duchess of Dove had the misfortune to meet the man in Jermyn Street who set in train the series of shocking events which came near to ruining the poor lady's good name. Since it is in the public interest that these events be made known, for they might happen to any one amongst us, this chronicle will relate them faithfully, but of course in a guarded way.

Mary Dove at the time of these events was thirty-one years of age. We have said that she was the quietest and shyest person imaginable, so that your heart quite went out to her. Now her shyness was Mary's cross, for conversation with strangers was positively an agony to her, while even with friends she could not divest her habit of mind of a reticence which she condemned in herself as an unnatural thing but which her friends never thought of but as refreshing. And weren't they right, when you think of the headaches you have had from listening to good talkers?

Any attempt to describe her classical features must be doomed to failure. Her reticence was as though mingled in the texture of her loveliness, and the flush of modesty seemed to light her complexion with an inner glow. Diffidence, and a profound respect for others' feelings, were in the very poise of the noticeably small head on her tall and slender figure. Nor was there anything about her manner to suggest the high confidence of fashion, though it must be admitted that she dressed remarkably well for a Duchess and that her legs were held in high esteem as being almost as good as an American chorus girl's. Her teeth were as white as boiled rice, but of course much nicer to look at. It has been said that her head was small. It was tiny. And it was crowned with a cluster of brown curls which she sometimes thought were unbecoming to the responsibilities of a widow of thirty-one, the mother of a schoolboy of ten, and the administratrix of large estates.

To make clear to the reader the horror of the misfortunes which were shortly to encompass this modest gentlewoman—for it is to her honour that she was that as well as a patrician—we shall have to touch briefly on the ordinary course of her life when in London. It should be stated at once that she was not "in society" as that term is understood by those who, no doubt for the best of reasons, live on its fringes.

To explain this anomaly we shall have to assume the burden of defining "society," and this can perhaps be best done by dividing it into three parts. Thus, the first part will be found to be made up of those who would not be seen dead in the illustrated papers, the second of those who week after week are seen dead in the illustrated papers, and the third of those who die before having managed to attract the notice of the illustrated papers.

The gentle Duchess of Dove was of the first part. The shady glamour of publicity had never touched her, her profile had not searched a million hearts, no photograph of her had ever been reproduced on a shiny page. For her shyness was as profound a fact of Mary Dove's being as Miss Garbo's reserve is in another sphere, while both would appear to have been more successful in evading the public attention than Sir James Barrie, whose modesty and shyness are known through his photographs and speeches throughout the world. But Mary's diffidence was to serve her a very dirty trick, as we shall see.

She lived in a large house in Grosvenor Square of so hideous an aspect and so inconvenient an interior that only difficulties of entail had prevented it from being sold or even given away to the first comer. A large part of her mornings was given over to dealing with her correspondence, which she did with the help of a distant female cousin who acted as her companion and secretary.

The name of this person was Miss Amy Gool, and she was the elder daughter of a baronet in reduced circumstances whose younger daughter had wisely married a hotel-proprietor of Bournemouth, with whom he lived in great content. This worthy baronet, who always enjoyed the best of health owing, as he often said, to the facts that "he stuck to whisky" and "took a spoonful of salts every morning," found that his declining years were clouded by an irritating perplexity. For he never could make up his mind in the mornings whether he would wear an Old Etonian tie or an I Zingari tie, and it so irritated him that he could not wear both at the same time that he was continually popping up to his bedroom to change the one for the other.

The Duchess's correspondence was a large one, for she was engaged in many public activities, such as presiding over committees to raise money for hospitals, finding employment for deserving young women, or furnishing clubs for the workless. It was seldom that she appeared publicly in these benevolent activities, owing to her shyness, and it was Miss Gool's duty to represent her. Thus the name of Amy Gool gradually became known as that of an intelligent philanthropist, much to the surprise of the charitable hotel-proprietor of Bournemouth, while it was sometimes said by the ill-informed that the Duchess of Dove and Oldham was not so active as she should be in furthering good works and thus ensuring the success of the Conservative Party at the next crisis in the affairs of the country.

Having thus directed Miss Gool in the execution of her duties, she would usually walk out to luncheon at the homes of friends in the neighbourhood or maybe now and then to Claridge's, a hotel which aims at and succeeds in combining elegance and respectability in such excellent measure that débutantes and dowagers can sit down in peace together. Cocktails are served, of course, if asked for, but a glass of sherry is more becoming both to the liveries of the attendants and the hats of the dowagers, in which feathers and other heirlooms are sometimes to be noted.

As is frequently the case, Mary Dove's favourite friend was a Mrs. Nautigale, who was as unlike herself as it is possible for one woman to be unlike another and still be part of the human race. This Mrs. Nautigale was a large and handsome woman who looked as though she had been constructed from materials at once more solid and formidable than those commonly used for less busy people. She was the wife of a retired shipowner who, making no secret of knowing what was good for him, spent most of his time in the country when she was in London and in London when she was in the country.

Mrs. Nautigale had a pronounced gift for collecting the most intimate friendships possible with men and women who could never quite overcome their surprise at having been collected. They then found themselves subjected to the alarming process of being pinned down, exhibited and fed in groups of not fewer than twenty, at which it was taken for granted that a good time was being had by all, though no one knew exactly why.

She was the soul of kindness, gave money freely to the rich, and had built her success as a hostess on having cleverly observed that there is no one like the distinguished Anglo-Saxon for enjoying a series of free meals provided that nothing, and particularly no conversation, is asked of him or her in return.

She also showed a tireless enthusiasm in visiting acquaintances who were ill in bed and who therefore, being unable to move freely, shortly found themselves to be amongst her oldest and most intimate friends. In golfing language it was said of this formidable lady that she hit from the inside out with a nice follow-through, while the very unkind among her regular guests said that Mrs. Nautigale reversed the usual procedure, for *her* friendships began in bed and continued to the dinner table. It should be clearly understood that such comments intended no reflections of any kind on the old girl's morality, for she was always the most properly conducted person imaginable, and took the view that a great deal of nonsense was talked about the pleasures of sin, since it was absurd to suppose that any woman could be enjoying herself in so untidy a situation.

No doubt it was due to Mary Dove's reticence and inability to assert herself that she was drawn towards her opposite. She came to rely greatly on Mrs. Nautigale's advice on all worldly matters, and if her son had so much as a cough she would at once telephone to her for the name of the best doctor, which Mrs. Nautigale would in due course supply from her collection of doctors. But such was her affection for the gentle Mary that Mrs. Nautigale, who would usually spare no trouble in arranging for her friends to be operated on as quickly as possible, would recommend her to consult only the less ferocious physicians of the day.

Amongst her friends it was only Mrs. Nautigale who could persuade Mary to go out in the evenings, and then very infrequently to parties or to balls but quietly to the play or the cinema, where she enjoyed respectively the lighter comedies and the most violent dramas. It should be added that twice every year she was honoured with a command to dine with their Majesties at Buckingham Palace. The unfortunate events to be related could not have come to pass if Mary had not spent nine out of every ten evenings at home, reading quietly or playing six pack bezique with her companion Amy Gool.

CHAPTER TWO

We come now to the distasteful task of appearing to cast aspersions on the reputation and character, as already described, of the Duchess of Dove and Oldham. That any man or woman could be so base as to assail the chastity of this lady is unthinkable. Yet any number did, and how.

We can do her friends and acquaintances the honour of stating emphatically that one in every ten disbelieved the first rumours that were set about, while the rest were stupefied at the disgraceful stories that were being whispered about the lady whom they had always esteemed as the most modest of her sex and the most virtuous of her generation. It is distressing to have to state that there were yet a few of the meaner sort who said that they had always wanted to have the low-down about her real character and that, now they had it, they weren't surprised a bit.

What were these rumours? What form did these disgraceful stories take? What, in a word, did the dicky-bird say?

It requires courage to write down such things, even in disbelief, of so modest a creature as Mary Dove. But the whispers were so very detailed and the stories so very exact that even her staunchest friends could not deny them substance.

To be brief, the lady was charged with deceit, hypocrisy, disloyalty to her class, her sex, the Conservative Party and the dignity of England, and of behaviour decidedly unbecoming to a gentlewoman. But there was worse to come. Incredible as it must seem, she was accused of using foul language, of unsuitable intimacy with men who had not been to public schools, of consorting with loose-livers generally, and of immorality in a big way.

It was said with every detail of particularity that on the many evenings when the Duchess of Dove was supposed to dine quietly at home with the unsuspecting Miss Gool and retire to bed shortly after ten o'clock, she in reality did nothing of the kind. Could deceit go further? Waiting only for her servants and her companion to retire, she slipped out of the house and went on the tiles.

But even then her behaviour would not have been so reprehensible had she been content to visit only the more reputable hotels and night-clubs and to dance and drink only with those of her acquaintance and station who were weak enough to seek distraction in such crowded places. But so pronounced, it appeared, was this so-called modest lady's malady that she must visit only the meaner night resorts, where the male guests were of decidedly questionable character, the ladies un-English in their manner of earning a living, and the laws against drinking after hours broken without so much as a thought to the bad example set by such law-breaking to the lower classes.

The Duchess of Dove had been seen not once but several times at such places. And if it is asked by whom she was recognised, it has to be admitted that she was not entirely alone in setting a bad example to the lower classes, though such of her friends who did this did it in a bunch together and not, like chaste Mary Dove, in company with pimps, panders and Communists.

But there was even worse to come. She had been seen drunk.

The evidence on this point was very particular and could not be entirely discounted merely because it came largely from women, as was only natural, since men are very properly reluctant to accuse ladies (of their own nationality) of the vice of drunkenness.

For instance, the evidence of Mrs. Gosoda was substantial, if spiteful. Now this Mrs. Gosoda was the widow of a theatrical magnate who, for long years a martyr to the chronic form of bankruptcy that pursues the illiterate in what is incorrectly called the Entertainment Business, had just before his death made a fortune in the gold boom of 1933-34. She had become a very well-known hostess amongst those who could not always rely on being invited to dine elsewhere, such as members of the Liberal Party, fashionable novelists, American bankers and foreigners not yet acclimatised. She was, however, progressing very favourably owing to a discovery she had recently made, that patricians were not averse to receiving tips.

Thus when she asked anyone over the courtesy rank of Honourable to dinner, a tiepin or bracelet was to be found beneath the napkin, while those who were invited on cruises in her yacht were always sent sufficient cash in plain envelopes to spend at ports of call and with which in their turn to tip Mrs. G.'s servants. Later she improved on this by giving each guest on landing at a foreign port money to spend in the currency of the country, as a marquess had complained of the loss sustained in exchanging the English banknotes she had given him.

Now one night this generous old party had conducted several of her dinner guests to an obscure night-club, just to show them the sights of the town, when to the horror and delight of her friends, who had heard much of the Duchess's beauty and inaccessibility, and of herself, who had often wondered if the Duchess would spend the week-end with her for less than a rope of pearls, there, on a divan in a corner for all the world to see, was the Duchess of Dove sitting between two young men whom even a provincial lady must have instantly recognised as bounders or Communists of the worst description. We have said that the Duchess was sitting between these types, but that does not convey the half of it, since she had her arm flung round the neck of one type and her hand on the knee of the other.

Such was Mrs. Gosoda's horror at this revolting spectacle that, her face wreathed in smiles, she darted across to the Duchess's table and twittered eagerly:

"Dear Duchess, how really nice to see you—and slumming too, just like us. Won't you and your friends join our party? They are all dying to meet you—and especially Crumwitch—*the* Crumwitch, you know, who flew in an aeroplane upside-down from London to Manchester, or perhaps it was to Liverpool."

Mrs. Gosoda's indignant testimony as to the reply she got to this kind invitation to meet Mr. Crumwitch was borne out by those members of her party who had edged nearer to the table. All agreed that the Duchess, while she looked even lovelier than she was always said to be, was evidently not herself. But what was most marked—in a lady so renowned for her diffidence—was the dirty look which she directed towards Mrs. Gosoda, who continued helplessly to twitter about this and that. Suddenly, however, the light of recognition appeared to awake in the Duchess's lovely grey eyes and the frozen look was replaced by one of unbecoming hilarity.

"Believe it or not," said the Duchess. "And who is old trout-face?"

"It's Mae West," cried one of the types beside her.

"No, it isn't," cried the other. "Mae West can take it. This one can dish it up, but she can't take it."

"Can't take what?" said the Duchess.

"Aren't I telling you?"

"But she can dish it up?"

"Are you telling me?" said the type.

"But *what* is it she can't take?" said the Duchess.

"You've only to look at her. Has she a sense of humour or not?"

"Oh, I see," said the Duchess. "But she *can* dish it up?"

"Didn't you hear her line of talk?" said the second type. "But she can't take it."

"Anyhow," said the Duchess, "I don't like her at all. Do you?"

Mrs. Gosoda, at last realising that her invitation was not being received in the spirit in which it had been given and that the Duchess had no intention of playing ball with her, was in the act of opening her mouth to express her disapproval when the Duchess deftly threw a green olive into it. The olives served in these low places, with the unsocial aim of stimulating thirst at unreasonable hours, are of an extreme hardness and should not be thrown at people. The types beside her, intensely amused by this beastly conduct, at once began pelting Mrs. Gosoda's party with the olives, so that they incontinently fled out of the place followed, to their indignation, by roars of drunken laughter.

CHAPTER THREE

It goes without saying that the reputation of the Duchess of Dove was such that it could for a considerable time withstand slanders and libels which would have ruined another in a day. Nor were there wanting a sufficient number of her friends, and notably Mrs. Nautigale to her honour, who stated emphatically that the stories were being spread about by the spirit of envy and by Reds.

Such statements were made the more credible by the spirit of unrest which was abroad in England at that time. For on the fall of the National Government the Fascists, merged at last into one body under Sir Oswald Mosley, had become the spearhead of the Conservative Party, Mosley had become Minister of War, and there were very many sound and far from silent Englishmen who believed heart and soul in the principles of Fascism, which are of course to take a strong stand and damn well keep it.

The Communists, however, had also greatly increased in numbers, were also eager to take a strong stand, and frequently did so in street battles with the Fascists, so that one did not know what law-abiding England was coming to. The spirit of unrest amongst the people was also aggravated and their disrespect towards the authorities increased by a series of horrible outrages which had lately been committed in London and which had inexplicably not been solved by the police.

It was this spirit of unrest which provoked Mrs. Nautigale, owning as she did an autographed photograph of Mussolini, to her statements that there was a fund at Moscow ear-marked just for spreading such scandalous stories in England with a view to disgracing the peerage, baronetage and knightage in the eyes of the people. Nor did she hesitate to use her influence on Lord Buick of Barstow, the most active if not the most powerful among her collection of newspaper peers, and one on whom she had frequently persuaded her favourite surgeons to operate for minor nervous disorders, to publish a series of well-informed articles on the menace of Red propaganda and the necessity for a stronger Air Force.

Now the one fact that is indisputable in this distressing affair is that the Duchess of Dove for many months did not know anything about it. This will not seem incredible to students of human nature, but if it does they will no doubt continue their studies with profit to themselves. Who will go up to a man and tell him that his wife has been taken in adultery? Will a girl's buddy break it to her that her adored fiancé is in reality a dirty old man? Will her best friend go to a woman and tell her that her husband is leading a double life? Certainly. But Mary Dove was a different cup of tea altogether. Her dignity, her character, her gentleness, stood so far above the nasty rumours about her that they could not be connected. Not even so intimate a friend as the formidable Mrs. Nautigale could ask her what she was up to. Indeed, there was really no possibility of warning Mary of the disgraceful scandals around her name, for not even her most cynical friends, who were quite ready to believe the worst of everyone, could bring themselves to believe when they were actually with her that she had any connection with the stories.

But what of Miss Amy Gool? Could she, when at last she heard of the stories, not have warned her friend and benefactor of the scandals that were so inexplicably being spread about her? But the fact remains that she did not, though in her favour it must be said that her attitude to the scandals had always been one of sharp incredulity. Miss Gool's face was one to which the expression of the sharper emotions came very easily, for she was not a woman who sought to charm. It is a curious fact, but one creditable to mankind at large, that in a world rank with spite the spiteful are not loved. Miss Gool was loved by no one except her Duchess, who said that people in general did not see her warmer side and that she was in reality a woman of the most generous instincts.

These generous instincts were not immediately perceptible to Mrs. Nautigale when she first told Amy Gool that Mary or Mary's double had been seen tipsy in a low night-club.

"Rot," said Miss Gool.

"Night before last," said Mrs. Nautigale.

"Piffle," said Miss Gool.

"Of course," said Mrs. Nautigale, who somehow seemed less formidable whenever she was with the secretary-companion. "But it's very worrying, all the same."

"What's worrying?"

"Why, these rumours."

"What rumours?"

Mrs. Nautigale explained what was being said about Mary since a month past, and added: "There are people who don't know Mary as well as we do and who are only too ready to get back on her for what they call her stand-offishness. Now, was she out at all that night?"

"No. She never goes out, except with you. In bed at ten."

"You're sure of that?"

"Of course I'm sure. I can't see through a closed door, naturally. And it isn't part of my duties to look through keyholes, Mrs. N. But the inference is that when a person goes into her bedroom at ten o'clock she is about to go to bed. My room is at the top of the house—in the attic, where I should be."

Mrs. Nautigale made no secret of being worried. Flatly disbelieving the stories as she did, she wished to disprove them by finding reliable witnesses who would swear that on such and such a night Mary had been safely tucked in bed.

"I see," she said thoughtfully, but then her old assurance returned as she added: "How stupid of me—of course, her maid can help."

"Help how?" said Amy Gool.

"Why, by assuring us that she sees Mary safely tucked up into bed every night."

"She doesn't. There's nothing Mary hates so much as anyone fussing around her when she is going to bed. And her maid is an incompetent ass, anyhow. I gave her notice yesterday."

"I see," said Mrs. Nautigale again. "Then there is actually nobody and nothing to prove that she could *not* slip out of the house at night after she has been seen going into her bedroom?"

"I never heard such rot," snapped Miss Gool. "Mary isn't the slipping sort—as anyone should know who isn't a fool."

"Now, Amy Gool, don't be so bumptious," said Mrs. Nautigale.

"I may be only a blister in Debrett," said Miss Gool, "but I'm not going to be called names by a woman whose fruity complexion can only be accounted for by immoderate drinking in secret."

Mrs. Nautigale, whose progress in society could only have been achieved by a victory of the mind over the senses and who therefore never heard what she did not want to hear, smiled with a vast amount of energy and said briskly: "Well, I shall be glad when August is here and Mary is safely at Dove. Then these silly stories *must* stop. But what to do in the meanwhile I really don't know. Perhaps Victor Wingless could help. Of course, you must know him well."

"He's a good man," said Miss Gool.

"Victor?" gasped Mrs. Nautigale.

"To hounds," said Miss Gool bitterly. "My advice to you, Mrs. Nautigale, is to leave well alone."

"But it's unbearable to have people saying such things about Mary. Now what do you think of this as a way out—to have the house watched at night just to prove that Mary is safely at home when someone looking like her is seen about with horrible people."

"I've never heard," said Miss Gool shrilly, "of anything so abominable. Have Mary watched? How dare you even suggest such a thing, Mrs. N.? Have *my* Mary watched?"

Mrs. Nautigale, who hated nothing so much as being called Mrs. N., looked at the companion with baffled curiosity. That the Gool had always been jealous of her benefactor's intimate friends, she had always known. Hitherto she had thought that this was due to the woman being a bitch of the first order and to knowing on which side her bread was buttered rather than to any impulse of real affection. But she could hardly doubt the reality of such affection now that the woman appeared to be on the verge of a nervous breakdown merely at the thought of any reflection on her beloved Mary.

"Of course, I didn't mean it in that way," said she. "I

needn't assure you, Amy Gool, that her friends wouldn't do anything in the world to hurt Mary in any way. Of course, you won't tell her anything about all this, will you?"

"Me?" said Miss Gool. "You're crazy."

"Well, really," said Mrs. Nautigale, and when she reached home she had to ring up a Cabinet Minister, two Ambassadors and several financiers before she could regain her customary feeling of assurance.

CHAPTER FOUR

But the companion had not swerved Mrs. Nautigale from her kindly purpose of giving the lie direct to the rumours about Mary. And here we come to the significant part played by Mr. Fancy in the shocking affair of the Duchess of Dove.

Henry James Fancy was a private enquiry agent who had been a detective-inspector at Scotland Yard attached to the Criminal Investigation Department. He had resigned this honourable post owing to a disagreement with the Assistant Commissioner, but this had reflected not at all either on his character or his ability, and he had left the force in an atmosphere of mutual good-will and respect. Mrs. Nautigale engaged the services of this incorruptible man, and the time was shortly to come when she was to wish that she hadn't.

Mr. Fancy was to watch the Duchess of Dove's house from ten o'clock in the evening until dawn, and he was to report to Mrs. Nautigale if he saw the Duchess leave the house. Mr. Fancy had been given a key into the gardens of Grosvenor Square, whence he could watch the house unobserved. His duties commenced on the night of Tuesday, June 9th. It is important to note this date.

On Tuesday and Wednesday he saw no one leave the house,

neither Duchess nor serving-maid. Yet late on Wednesday night the Duchess of Dove and Oldham was reported to have been seen at a coffee-stall in Limehouse with two male types, all of them the worse for drink. We can imagine Mrs. Nautigale's relief at this news, for Mr. Fancy's testimony would prove that there must be someone trying to impersonate the Duchess to the detriment of her reputation. To make doubly sure, however, she instructed the detective to continue his watching on Thursday night—June 11th. It is very important to note this date, so forget the previous one.

At a quarter-to-one that night Mr. Fancy telephoned to Mrs. Nautigale's bedside, according to her instructions, and informed her that her Grace had left the house ten minutes before and had walked rapidly away towards Bond Street. Mr. Fancy had followed her. At the corner of Davies Street and Claridge's her Grace had stepped into a Daimler limousine driven by a chauffeur in dark livery which had instantly whirled her away towards Oxford Street. Mr. Fancy had been unable to follow for lack of a convenient taxi, but he had taken down the number of the limousine, which, however, was shortly to turn out to be that of a car from a hiring company.

Now here the excellent Mrs. Nautigale found herself in a really monstrous predicament. What the devil was she to do? It was now evident that her beloved Mary, her lovely and gentle Mary, was the victim of a peculiar and vicious malady. Was she mad? Was she bewitched? Had she gone cuckoo? Or had she fallen under some horrible man's influence who, with the aid of hypnotism or of drugs, had divided the foundations of her character into those of Dr. Jekyll and Mr. Hyde?

It was unthinkable that her modest and diffident Mary could be in her right senses on the nights she left home so furtively. The hypocrisy, the deceit, the drunkenness! And in such company, in actual contact with such low types. Mrs. Nautigale, to her honour, did not for a moment admit the possibility that her dear Mary had, throughout their long friendship, concealed beneath her lovely and modest exterior the lusts of a wanton. No, there must be some explanation.

Now it will be obvious to the clear-thinking that Mrs. Nautigale here made a grave mistake. On the very day after Mr. Fancy's report she should have gone to Mary, should have frankly told her of the disgraceful stories and of the fact that she had actually been seen leaving the house at night, and she should have implored her to leave London at once for a long stay at Dove Park before her reputation was irreparably damaged. Now had Mrs. Nautigale done this, she would have been astonished at Mary's answer and gratified by her instant compliance. And she would in all probability have averted the catastrophe.

The only excuse we can find for the old girl does credit to her heart, if not to her judgment. She hesitated because she simply could not bring herself to believe that there was not somewhere some explanation which would instantly exonerate her dear Mary—if only one could find it. Therefore she instructed Mr. Fancy to stay on the job, and thus precipitated the catastrophe which is still remembered whenever mention is made of the peerless Duchess of Dove.

For on the morning of June 19th an elderly man of determined but genteel appearance, and a manner very subdued as though by long meditation on abstract matters, called at the house in Grosvenor Square and asked if he might be permitted to see her Grace. Since his card bore the name Superintendent G. I. Crust, the butler, an elderly person called Hebblethwaite, immediately showed him into the small study downstairs in the certainty that Mr. Crust was calling in connection with a police charity in which her Grace was interested.

When Mary, followed by Miss Gool, entered the room—evidently on their way out of the house for a walk—the Superintendent's manner was so very subdued that his words were quite inaudible. Mary looked helplessly towards her companion, who said: "Speak up, man, speak up. We were just going out for a walk, so I hope you won't keep us long."

At this moment Mary's dog, a Sealyham known as Algy, and on whose insistence this walk was being taken, came in and protested loudly at the presence of a bulky stranger. It was, therefore, in a voice much less subdued that Superintendent Crust had to state his business, which was to the effect that he would be very glad and that the Commissioner of Police would be very glad if her Grace would be kind enough to go with him to Scotland Yard in connection with some enquiries which the police found themselves compelled to make.

"I have," said Superintendent Crust who, like a good policeman of the old school, would yield not even to the very best novelists of the new school an enviable capacity for using three long words where one short one would do, "I have a conveyance outside. And I shall endeavour," said he, "to make you comfortable, your Grace."

Mary, her shyness for the moment dissipated by bewilderment at being talked to in this way, looked blankly from the Superintendent to her companion.

"Will you kindly explain," said Miss Gool severely, "what exactly you are talking about? And try—don't endeavour—to use ordinary plain English, if you can."

Superintendent Crust's depression grew visibly. He was, as he said later to his wife, the last person in the world to have an eye for a pretty woman, but the Duchess's beauty was of a kind to knock a man all of a heap. So he preferred, in the execution of his duty, to concentrate his gaze on the displeasing face of Miss Gool—which was, as he tactlessly pointed out to Mrs. Crust, much more the kind of face he was used to.

"I want," he said despondently, "her Grace to come with me to Scotland Yard. I—we want to ask her some questions."

"Questions," Mary sighed. "Me? Whatever for?"

"Your Grace," said the Superintendent, "explanations will be forthcoming in due course."

"He means," Miss Gool translated, "that he'll tell you later."

"But tell me what?" asked Mary.

"What," Miss Gool interpreted to the Superintendent, "is the nature of the explanations which will be forthcoming in due course?"

"Madam," said poor Crust, "we shall exercise all possible courtesy. I ask her Grace to accompany me in her own best interests. We have not taken out a warrant."

"A *what?*" said Miss Gool.

"Warrant," said the Superintendent miserably.

At this point Mary rose to her feet. To have said that she was very shy does not mean she was without that matchless confidence of breeding which can dismiss without offence. Algy, yapping around her feet, ran between her and the door in high expectation of his walk.

"I'm afraid," said she, "I must go for my walk now, Inspector. Please excuse me. I will leave Miss Gool with you, as she attends to all business matters for me. Good-morning."

Superintendent Crust, now also on his feet, was sweating—or, as he put it later, perspiring—with discomfort.

"Your Grace," said he, "I am afraid I shall have to ask you to come with me."

Miss Gool threw herself across the room and prodded the Superintendent in the chest with her handbag.

"Have to! Have to? Are you daring—daring—to suggest that the Duchess is being charged with something?"

Mary, her tall slender figure swaying just a little where she stood, said quietly: "Leave the poor man alone, Amy." Her enormous grey eyes were very steady as she addressed the Superintendent.

"Please explain," said she, "what it is you want to ask me questions about."

As poor Mr. Crust began drawing on his reserves of comforting understatements Miss Gool gave him a really sharp prod in the kidneys with the sharp handle of her bag.

"Here!" said he.

"The Duchess has asked you," Miss Gool snapped, "what you want to ask her questions about. Why not answer—or respond to—her?"

"Oh, all right," said the Superintendent wearily. "Murder."

CHAPTER FIVE

Now it is obvious that a great deal must have gone before this, for even in these times of equal opportunity for women it is not every day that a duchess is suspected of the crime of murder. Therefore we must return to that incorruptible man, Henry James Fancy. For it was Mr. Fancy's lifelong passion for putting two and two together that had brought Mary Dove to this tragic pass.

It has already been said that the political unrest of the times had been aggravated by certain unsolved crimes of violence. During that spring and summer there had been two atrocious murders in London. We shall not go into them in detail. It was at once evident to the investigators that there was a connection between these two crimes, both from the parallel situation of the victims and the similarity between the murderer's methods.

The Fulham Road Murder, so called from the fact that it took place in Redcliffe Road, was discovered early on the morning of April 17th. The Shepherd Market Murder came to light early on the morning of May 10th. Both victims were young men, the one a shop assistant and the other a bank clerk, who lived alone in lodgings. In each case the youth was discovered naked on his bed, naturally much disarranged, and with the head almost severed from the body by an inhuman slash across the throat from ear to ear. There were other mutilations of a fanciful nature which it will serve no purpose to describe. No weapon was found in either lodging. There were further similarities: a faint perfume, agreeable rather than sickly, much to the surprise of the detectives, who had been brought up to believe that all perfumes were sickly: and cigarette ends with the clearly-defined marks of lip rouge.

It was, therefore, impossible not to suppose that a woman was responsible for these inhuman crimes. Against this there had to be set the medical experts' view that the murders and mutilations had been committed not only with the same knife but with a special type of short and narrow surgical knife commonly sold only to members of the surgical profession.

Exhaustive enquiries had given the police no clue as to the young men's movements or companions during the hours before they met their deaths. Neither had been seen returning to his lodgings. The police had, therefore, to come to the conclusion that these two unfortunate young men had fallen victims to the unspeakable lusts of a madwoman, who had accosted them or had been accosted by them in the streets.

Since it was, of course, obvious that this female fiend could not be an Englishwoman, there was much discussion as to her probable nationality. Opinion finally settled on Germany or Japan as her land of origin, both of those countries being at that time on strained commercial terms with England. The popular newspapers lost no time in labelling these crimes as the "Jane the Ripper Murders."

In almost every major particular the third hideous outrage of the Jane the Ripper series was identical with the two preceding ones. The abominations of sexual depravity were again evident. The young man, a bookmaker's clerk and a member of the British Fascist Party, lived alone in lodgings. Once again the murderess had been at pains to leave behind her the faint and agreeable odour of her perfume and the rouge-tipped cigarette ends, which were of a kind largely smoked by the less fastidious sort—in England, it should be added, rather than in Germany and Japan. Once again the police were puzzled by the discrepancy between the perfume, which an expert in odours had pronounced to be that of an expensive French scent made by Monsieur Coty of Paris, and therefore unlikely to be that of a woman of the streets, and the cigarette ends of a type commonly smoked by such unfortunates. Moreover, there was again the probability that the third crazy murder, like the previous two, had been committed by someone not unfamiliar with the practical uses of a surgical knife.

But it is the date of the third Jane the Ripper atrocity—known as the Percy Street Murder from the fact that it happened a few hundred yards away in Charlotte Street—which must command our attention. It was discovered by the woman who "did" for the unfortunate young man at half-past seven in the morning of Friday, June 12th.

Now it will be remembered that it was on the night of

Thursday the 11th that the conscientious Mr. Fancy had seen the Duchess of Dove slip unseen—or so she must have thought—out of her house and ride away in a hired limousine towards Oxford Street.

But he had not seen her return, though he had watched the house until dawn. Yet of the fact that she had returned in the course of the night there could be no doubt, for Mrs. Nautigale had telephoned to her and spoken with her at half-past eight in the morning, when the Duchess had complained of a slight headache from having slept too heavily.

There were no other entrances to the house than the front door and the area door, both of which had been under Mr. Fancy's conscientious eye throughout the night. Then how had she managed to get back without having been spotted by him? And exactly the same thing happened again on the following Wednesday night, June 17th. The question as to how the Duchess returned to her house unseen by him under his very nose upset and irritated Mr. Fancy to such a degree that his passion for putting two and two together was, if possible, increased.

But when he had made the addition even this incorruptible man was appalled by the conclusion to which it appeared to lead him.

He did not follow the Duchess on this second occasion, intent only on solving the mystery of her return and fearing that she might give him the slip while he followed her and re-enter the house before he could get back to his post. She was not this time in evening dress but in a dark coat of some light clinging material and a small dark hat with a narrow brim coming low down over her eyes. He saw her walk swiftly across Grosvenor Square towards Carlos Place.

Now Carlos Place is not far from the historic and once secluded defile known as Lansdowne Passage. And it was on that night, Wednesday, June 17, that there took place the fourth and only unsuccessful Jane the Ripper crime.

At two o'clock in the morning a young man of the Jewish persuasion entered Lansdowne Passage from the Berkeley Street end. While that fashionable thoroughfare was not without the movement of motor-cars flirting with the two entrances of the May Fair Hotel, Lansdowne Passage lay deserted before young Mr. A. Candlenose, for it was under that name he preferred to be known in the exercise of his profession, which was that of a ventriloquist.

He hastened his walk, not from timidity, but because he was sleepy and wished to get home to his room in Ducking Pond Mews, near Hertford Street. Half-way down the Passage, and just past that point in one high wall of the narrow defile which, once the boundary of the spacious Devonshire House estate, is now broken by the kitchen entrance of the May Fair Hotel, his ears noted a faint echo of his own ringing footsteps.

Mr. A. Candlenose's recollection of the immediately subsequent events was clouded. He had no more than just noted that the light hurrying footsteps behind him were growing fainter as they approached, as is the case when people start to run on their toes, and he was in the act of turning his head to glance over his shoulder, when a woman's gloved and scented hand was clapped very strictly over his mouth from behind, his head was wrenched back with ferocious suddenness, so that he must have lost his balance and fallen but for the soft lithe body of his assailant behind him, and a knife was slashed sharply across his throat.

Mr. A. Candlenose could remember no more. He was positive that the attack could not have lasted as long as two seconds in all. He saw the flash of the knife—a short one, he fancied—almost at the same instant as his head was wrenched back by the cruelly tight hand over his mouth. He admitted, in point of fact, that the perfumed hand had given him such a turn that he had closed his eyes tight and given himself up for lost. This was understandable, for perfume had been much on men's minds since the first Jane the Ripper crime, and more than one wretched woman had recently been assaulted for using scent. And rightly.

Thus the Semitic but unfortunate ventriloquist saw nothing of his assailant. But he was positive, from the pressure of his back and shoulder-blades against the supporting body behind, that he had been attacked by a tall skinny sort of woman with firm girlish breasts. Mr. A. Candlenose said this with a certain relish, for he had frequently been mocked by his friends on his preference for the more ample ladies of their acquaintance. In the future this preference was to become an obsession.

It was fortunately a policeman, returning to the police-station at Vine Street from his beat in the neighbourhood of Curzon Street, who found the unconscious young man lying face-downwards against a wall of the deserted Passage. While the victim had lost a great deal of blood from the terrible gash across his throat, and his condition was precarious, he owed his life to the fact that he was that day wearing a hard collar instead of a soft one. Jane the Ripper had been in too great a hurry to note that her knife, after severing the left-side veins of the throat, had been deflected by the collar, which had been cleanly cut across.

Mr. Fancy read the reports of this brutal and senseless attempt on Mr. A. Candlenose's life in the evening papers of that Friday. There was one significant addition to what has been related above. The policeman who found the ventriloquist had, on his approach towards the blind end of Curzon Street which gives only to the narrow aperture of

Lansdowne Passage, noted but one person coming from that direction. This was a tall and slender woman walking with great haste who, on passing him, had turned left into Bolton Street. Her features had been concealed not only by the brim of her black hat but by the fact that she kept her head down, as though preoccupied only with her haste to get home. She had worn a long black coat of some flimsy material which could have "afforded," so the constable reported, "a suitable place of concealment for the alleged weapon with which the assault was committed."

Now this is not the place in which to follow in detail the processes of Mr. Fancy's upright mind after he had digested these and similar reports. He very properly tried to put away from him every consideration but that of his duty to his fellow-citizens. It should be added that he took no pride whatsoever in being the first man to be able to point the finger of evidence against the lady—if so hideous a criminal, whether duchess or queen, could be called a lady—who had committed these murders. His duty first and foremost was to prevent any more such crimes, and therefore it lay not in reporting his conclusions to Mrs. Nautigale but to the proper authorities. And so, with his matchless flair for making himself a confounded nuisance to his betters, Henry James Fancy went with his report to Scotland Yard.

CHAPTER SIX

At this time Major-General Sir Giles Prest-Olive was Commissioner of Metropolitan Police and the Hon. Basil Icelin was Assistant Commissioner in charge of the Criminal Investigation Department. Since all the crisp mumbo-jumbo of the detective writer's craft must be as boring for the reader to read as it is for the chronicler to write, we shall call them Prest-Olive and Icelin. We shall also try to refer to Scotland Yard, the Big Five, the dictaphone, the radio patrol, the Maxim silencer, the ballistics expert, the Flying Squad, finger-prints, and the crime reporter as seldom as may be, though of course you can't keep a good man down.

Sir Giles Prest-Olive's was entirely a political appointment on the formation of the Conservative-Fascist Cabinet after the fall of the National Government, and was never intended to be anything but temporary, though it turned out to be even more temporary than was anticipated, as we shall see. He was a very good chap, and Basil Icelin was, of course, an excellent chap—*the* Icelin who won the Amateur in 192– and was runner-up in the Open in 193–.

Prest-Olive's iron-grey appearance was so very distinguished that even when seen full-face he appeared to be a clean-cut profile largely made up of a fine aristocratic nose. It was no doubt this fine nose that had steered him so comfortably through the sedentary life of a successful soldier, for in England it is wisely recognised that to a Staff Officer good looks must matter very much more than they should to a mere actor with a painted face. It was of General Prest-Olive that Maréchal Foch was reported to have said: "It is soldiers like Prest-Olive who almost unite the English and French armies in affection for the Belgians." His wife was one of the Leicestershire ffox-Vermins, and he had to like it.

Basil Icelin, who had won his position by merit—although of course he was a good chap, too—was a dark, lean fellow with a somewhat sardonic expression. Unlike Prest-Olive he did not look at all "typically" English, which was surprising, since he was also an Irishman. Had Icelin not been so very good at games—he had also played cricket for Oxford and Kent—he might sometimes have been suspected of sarcasm.

Even as it was, some thought that his views on cricket and war were unsound.

While Superintendent Crust was making his call on the Duchess of Dove, these two men sat in Prest-Olive's office and stared at one another across a wide table stacked high with all the papers (usually known in crisp English as *dossier*) relating to the Jane the Ripper series of crimes. On the very top was Henry James Fancy's report, which had been read with respectful attention, for Fancy had always been known in the department as a conscientious headache. Moreover, his report had since been supplemented by routine police investigations. The motor-car hiring company owning the limousine in which the Duchess was seen on the night of Thursday the 11th reported that the car had been hired over the telephone by a man's voice: that the lady who had entered the car at the corner of Davies Street had instructed the driver to drop her at the corner of Oxford Street and Tottenham Court Road: that he had done so and been paid his fee and that he knew no more about his fare.

But much more than that had been done by the C.I.D. under Icelin's capable direction, and they now knew almost as much about certain aspects of the case as the public did. For example, the police had established that during the last four months the Duchess's mode of life had changed in the most peculiar way, but only at night. Her first appearance as a high-flier had been traced to a night two weeks before the first Jane the Ripper murder near the Fulham Road. Detectives had interviewed the proprietors of the mean night resorts at which she was said to have been seen. These men, whose eagerness to help the police was a touching tribute to the laws of England, had immediately identified the Duchess from snapshots recently taken when she was walking with her Sealyham in Hyde Park. Of course they had not known she was the Duchess of Dove and had placed her as a classy tart and hot number. Moreover, two of them and the keeper of a coffee-stall had identified a photograph of the victim of the second Jane the Ripper crime, known as the Shepherd Market Murder, as that of a young man who had been seen on two occasions with the hot number and who had made no concealment of the fact that he had been "gone on" her. The police had hitherto been unable to establish any such direct connection between the Duchess and the other two murdered young men.

"But what we've got," Icelin summed up, "seems to be quite enough."

Icelin's sardonic expression was very much in evidence that morning. Trained as he had been by such highly capable Commissioners of Police as Trenchard and his successor Waldo-Huish, he was heartily sick of his present chief's gentlemanly anxiety to do the pukka thing. But Icelin was an understanding kind of man and forgave much to a poor devil who had had the courage to marry one of the Leicestershire ffox-Vermins, teeth and all.

Prest-Olive was looking extremely worried, as well he might. Crime was one thing, and a duchess was another. Stood England where it did? Poor Prest-Olive thought it extremely unlikely, and he knew jolly well he didn't, for this Jane the Ripper business was forcing his resignation.

"What a stink," he sighed, "this will make."

"Has made," said Icelin the precise.

"You got nothing from the servants at the Grosvenor Square house?"

"They quite obviously know nothing. Her personal maid, who left some days ago, is being traced. But I fancy that won't help us. The servants all combine in loving their mistress and loathing Miss Gool."

"Perhaps," said Prest-Olive hopefully, "this Gool person, out of hatred for the Duchess, has been impersonating her. Worth looking into, Icelin."

"Is it?" said Icelin. "No amount of disguise could make Miss Gool either resemble the Duchess, look like a hot number, or help her to lure young men into her clutches. Unless, that is, young men have changed a lot since my time."

Prest-Olive, almost whimpering with exasperation, said: "But where's the motive, Icelin? How could a woman like that change into such a fiend?"

"Don't ask me, sir. I'm not married."

Then his chief, remembering himself, became a forceful Kipling character.

"Damn it, Icelin," said he, "this is as nasty a case as we've ever had. You'll agree it isn't one of plain murder?"

"These killings," said Icelin sourly, "have certainly not been done by someone with a respect for good form and the dear old Alma Mater, if that's what you mean, sir."

"You know very well what I mean," snapped Prest-Olive, who very properly deplored all jokes about serious subjects like public schools. "These," he said severely, "are maniacal murders——"

"And sexual," said Icelin.

"Oh, come—that's only theory."

"Better read the doctors' reports, sir. There is no doubt about it being business after pleasure with Jane the Ripper."

"Then that is why," snapped Prest-Olive, "it is quite impossible to connect the Duchess with these crimes."

"Quite," said Icelin. After all, the ffox-Vermin kind of mind was often right. "Quite. She might have murdered the poor wretches but could never, never have tucked up with them. It's quite a point, sir."

"It's a big point," said Prest-Olive.

"If you say so. Though one has heard of a queen having a rough-and-tumble with corporals."

"Not an English queen, Icelin."

"Of course not, sir. We have always had a sense of proportion."

"May I ask what that means?"

"The corporal is promoted."

"I fancy you must be a little off-colour to-day, Icelin. Where is this discussion leading us?"

"Well," smiled Icelin, "to the House of Lords. No psychological flummery can get us away from the fact that what evidence we *have* got about Jane the Ripper points directly at the Duchess of Dove."

Prest-Olive said: "It might be faked. It must be faked. Icelin, here is one of the best-bred and loveliest women in the world——"

"So was Messalina."

"I am not talking about a Frenchwoman, Icelin, but about the most gracious lady in England. And it is not credible that she can be a murderess. I say there is something damned queer about this case, for you and I know in our hearts that such a woman could not be capable of these crimes."

Icelin said: "Look here, sir, I want to arrest the lady as little as you do." He flicked a finger at the papers on the table. "But here is the evidence, and all we have to put against it is that this might be a Jekyll and Hyde case, and that is *not* evidence."

"But you agree that we can't arrest her at this stage?"

"Are you asking me as a policeman or a politician?"

"Heavens above, Icelin, can't we be just human for a change?"

"Oh, as a human being I can see the Home Secretary's point that it would be a highly disturbing factor in the present mood of the people to arrest the Duchess of Dove as Jane the Ripper."

"Exactly." Prest-Olive picked up the telephone. "I am going to ask Wingless to lunch. You might come, too. He is a relation of hers and a chap with shrewd ideas."

"First-rate golfer," Icelin commented.

Prest-Olive left a message for Colonel Wingless at his club. Then Superintendent Crust came in.

Icelin said: "You look worn out, Crust."

"I am that, sir." He addressed the Commissioner, who was running a comb through his charming iron-grey hair. "Her Grace is here, sir. With her companion. Perfectly ready to answer anything you like to ask her. I've had them shown into Mr. Icelin's room."

Icelin was childishly relieved when his chief said that he would see her himself. He knew that the interview would be quite profitless and at the same time harrowing. It was only his irritation with Prest-Olive's deference to social values that had made him emphasise the weight of the evidence against the Duchess. There was something inexplicably queer about this case which made him positive that the solution would not be found through ordinary police methods. That was why he had welcomed the approaching interview with Victor Wingless.

Then he noticed that Crust had brought out something small and white from his pocket and was now looking down at it in a very despondent way. Prest-Olive was combing his iron-grey moustache.

Icelin said: "Look."

Both men stared at poor Crust with a distaste which they knew was unfair. He had done no more than his duty. Both quite consciously tried to shut their sense of smell against the faint agreeable perfume that came from the soft white thing in Crust's large hand.

Then he very gently put the flimsy handkerchief on a corner of the large table. Neither Prest-Olive nor Icelin made any attempt to touch it. The tiny coronet with the strawberry leaves seemed to be as big as the room. As the handkerchief was now almost under their noses it was quite impossible not to identify Jane the Ripper's perfume.

"She dropped it," said the Superintendent sulkily, "while picking up her dog—a Sealyham."

Crust went out. Icelin thoughtfully folded the handkerchief and placed it in an envelope.

Prest-Olive said: "My God, where's this going to end? The next thing will be that we'll find a mutilated corpse clutching a hair from a Sealyham."

CHAPTER SEVEN

Now the part played by Colonel Wingless in the tragic affair of the Duchess of Dove has hitherto remained obscure to historians. No doubt he owes this neglect to his appearance, which was that of a two-bottle man and, therefore, not compatible with that of a psychologist of first-rate ability.

Wingless was a tall and powerful-looking man with a heavy, handsome face notable for its high colour, which was described by those who disliked him as fruity and by his friends as ruddy. His eyes were of that cold blue sometimes approved by lady novelists and nautical enthusiasts as "frozen" or "chilled" blue, as of men inured to hardships on the seven seas, although the impression they give might be more accurately described as one of rugged and impenetrable vacancy. This impression Wingless had found to be an invaluable disguise for a man of average attainments in fields where looking silent and beefy wasn't everything. Since leaving the army, in which he had always been known as "a soldier with a future," whatever that may mean, he had won his way to the managing-directorship of one of the largest aircraft-building concerns in England.

It was said of Wingless that the honour of having done the bravest action of the 1914-18 war must fall to him. In the autumn of '15, miraculously unhurt after more than a year in the trenches, he was in London on short leave. Walking in mufti down Piccadilly one morning, he was handed a white feather by a large woman with the cold eyes of one who is kind to animals but to no one else. But Wingless was larger and, deftly grabbing her by the waist, he turned her over and gave her several resounding smacks on her behind. When charged with common assault at Marlborough Street he had explained that the lady had looked such a tough baby that he had wanted to find out if she had hair on her chest. Fined £5. Acclaimed as a hero by all his fellow-officers and men on his return to France, he had quickly showed himself at heart a slave to convention by winning the Victoria Cross.

After luncheon he listened intently to Prest-Olive's worried and far from precise summary of the facts collected by the police about the Jane the Ripper crimes. Then he turned to Icelin, whose thin intellectual face was something of a refreshment for the eyes against the background of bewildered near-Nordics in the club smoking-room.

"Icelin, did you get anything at all from your interview with her this morning?"

"The chief saw her alone."

Basil Icelin's deep eyes twinkled just perceptibly as he said this, and Wingless smiled faintly in return. Prest-Olive was lighting a cigar. Both men knew the poor man's weakness for a lady of title, and if the occasion had not been so tragic Wingless must have smiled outright at the vision of Prest-Olive's deferential bedside manner at the examination of a Duchess on a disagreeable matter of three atrocious murders.

"Nothing," said the iron-grey Commissioner. He spoke, when he thought of it, in clipped speech, though being a naturally garrulous man he did not always think of it. "Not one thing. I never saw—hope never to see again—such horror and bewilderment on a woman's face. She knew nothing—could give no explanation."

"That," said Icelin dryly, "was only to be expected. The person responsible for three senseless murders would naturally be hard put to it to give a reasonable explanation."

Prest-Olive became all profile and gave a snort. He disapproved of sarcasm, except about Jews and foreigners, and sometimes wondered how Icelin had ever managed to win the Amateur.

"Icelin," said Wingless, "do you believe she did it?"

Slightly shaking his head, Icelin said: "But that's neither here nor there. I'm only a policeman, and it's not my job to have views but to collect facts and present them with the body of the accused to a judge and jury."

"And you think you have enough evidence?"

"Unfortunately—yes."

"What about the gaps? For instance, this chap Fancy saw her go out on the two nights in question but didn't see her return. But we know for a fact that she was in her bed early in the morning because Doris Nautigale spoke to her on the telephone. If it really *was* the Duchess who went out it's impossible she could have returned without Fancy's eagle eye spotting her. Therefore it was not the Duchess who went out. What about that?"

"Not much," said Icelin. "The important point is that

Fancy saw her or her exact double go out. For all we care officially she might have got back on a broomstick."

"Another point is," said Wingless slowly, "that Mary has never smoked a cigarette in her life."

Prest-Olive's handsome profile brightened at this, but Icelin was less easily impressed.

"No more than a few months ago," he said, "the lady in question never went out to night clubs in queer company and never did a great many things which she—apparently—has been doing recently. Then why should it be so improbable that she has also taken to smoking cheap cigarettes? In fact, Wingless, it isn't improbable—given the very peculiar atmosphere of this whole case."

"Look here," Wingless said, "I don't believe that Mary Dove is a murderess, Prest-Olive doesn't believe it, and you don't believe it either. But we all know that it's only in books that people can be impersonated and disguised so perfectly. Icelin, do you believe in perfect disguises?"

"Do I believe in sea serpents? Go on."

"I gather the Home Secretary agrees with Prest-Olive that it would be unwise at this stage to make any move against the Duchess or any statement to the Press. Now let me suggest a plan. I shall persuade Mary to go into a nursing-home to-day or to-morrow. Old Dr. Lapwing will have charge of her, and she will be under observation day and night. Then should any hint of your suspicions against so prominent a person as the Duchess leak out, and should it be said that the police are conspiring to defeat the ends of justice by not arresting her, you will have a fairly good answer in the fact that she is in a nursing-home. And if there is another Jane the Ripper murder while she's there, you will have a decisive answer. Now I suppose it has occurred to you two blokes that we shall only find a clue to the real criminal when we trace the owner of the male voice which hired the car on the night of the Charlotte Street Murder."

Icelin said: "Congratulations, Wingless. The use of a surgical knife and the male telephone voice are, in point of fact, the only items in the whole damn business at all favourable to the Duchess. We can't hope to trace them, of course. But they do help us to form a point of view which isn't—speaking impersonally—entirely hostile to her." He turned to Prest-Olive. "What do you think of the nursing-home idea?"

"Excellent," said Prest-Olive, who had already decided he would call on the Duchess at the nursing-home and maybe be asked to stay for a cup of tea. Would it be correct to take his wife? He added: "What we have to fear, Icelin, is even the smallest leakage to the Press about what the police know or suspect."

"Believe me," said Wingless grimly, "one little leak will cause a flood."

CHAPTER EIGHT

Now Wingless's mind was an obstinate one, and it had fixed on two points: first, the male voice which had hired the car: second, that the murderess must be unusually familiar with the routine of poor Mary's daily life.

One could dismiss the possibility of Jane the Ripper being one of the domestic staff at the house in Grosvenor Square, for there was not a woman among them except Mary herself who could even remotely fit the bill as to face and figure. The dismissed maid was fair, plump, and a good head shorter. And if there was one certainty in the whole wretched business it was that the beautiful woman who had been seen and recognised by Mrs. Gosoda and others was *not* a man impersonating a woman.

Then where, he asked Mrs. Nautigale later that afternoon, did the man's voice come in? Not that the good lady was listening, for she was in the greatest state of rage imaginable. Only an hour or so before she had heard from Amy Gool of the visit to Scotland Yard that morning. From Miss Gool's brief recital, marked by strong disapproval of police procedure as a whole, one could only imagine that Mary was lucky not to have been clapped into prison then and there. And Mrs. Nautigale's horror at anyone even daring to suspect any connection whatever between her gentle Mary and a murderess was for the time being submerged by her wrath with the Commissioner of Police for being such a fathead. The idiocy! The impudence! Why, only the day before she had invited the Prest-Olives to dine on Thursday week to meet the new German Ambassador, Count Musselsaroffsir.

When exasperated, Mrs. Nautigale always turned to the telephone. She rang up Lady Prest-Olive. She told her that she had just heard that her husband was a mental defective. And she regretted, she said, having to cancel her invitation for dinner on Thursday week owing to an unreasonable prejudice amongst her friends against dining with a man who might at any moment think he was the Emperor of Jerusalem. Doing this had given Mrs. Nautigale a small measure of satisfaction, for she could imagine the ripe dressing-down which that horse-faced creature of a ffox-Vermin snob would give her handsome nitwit of a husband that evening when he got home.

"I hope," she had said to Amy Gool, "you told them what you thought of them."

"I surprised them," said Miss Gool.

Thus it was a Mrs. Nautigale even more determined than

usual whose collaboration Colonel Wingless was seeking. She offered it very gladly, expressing only the regret, as they drove to Mary's house, that Basil Icelin was not married, as she would have liked to put a spoke in his wheel, too.

"You might," said Wingless, "steal his mashie-niblick. That would get him on the raw."

"Do be serious, Victor."

"Try it and see how serious Icelin will be."

They found Mary in her bedroom. She was reclining on a sofa by the window, and though the day was very warm a Cashmere shawl was thrown loosely over her. Miss Gool went out as they came in. Poor Mary looked very white after her ordeal. She tried to smile a greeting to her friends, but the smile was shattered by a sob. And she stared at them helplessly with eyes so horrified and haunted that Mrs. Nautigale's own instantly filled with tears. Indeed, the thought of any connection between the gentle and lovely woman on the sofa and the fiend known as Jane the Ripper was so hideously insulting to the very dignity of human beings in general that Wingless himself had all he could do to pretend he was suffering from nothing more than a little catarrh.

Mary said: "Doris—Victor—why didn't you tell me months ago of the things that were being said about me?"

"Dear," cried Mrs Nautigale. "I knew, you see, they weren't *true.* What was the use of hurting you? I thought they must come to an end by themselves. Dearest Mary, no one who knows you ever thought—or thinks—of them except as horrible lies. Victor?"

"I agree," said Wingless, again clearing his throat.

Mary said: "They can't be just lies."

She was so calm and reasonable that Mrs. Nautigale's tears fell faster than ever.

"A lie," Mary said, "is a word. But this isn't a word."

"Why, dear, of course they are lies."

"A lie is a word. But this is a body."

"Why, Mary, whatever do you mean?"

"There is someone or something in this world who has my body and my face and my eyes and my voice. How can that be a 'lie'?"

"But, darling——"

Mary said: "There is a spirit of more than human evil in a body which is the twin of mine. And this thing has my face and my eyes and my voice. O God, what shall I do? What *can* I do?"

"Look here, Mary," Wingless said, "the police think that——"

Mary said: "The police? I'm afraid, Victor, that the police haven't been trained to arrest spirits. And after all," she said reasonably, "it's in the Bible, isn't it, that even God Himself couldn't really arrest Satan, so what can we expect a poor policeman to do?"

"He arrested him," said Mrs. Nautigale severely, "and threw him into Hell."

"You could hardly call that solitary confinement, could you, Doris? Do you know what I think, Victor? I think I am being punished for my pride and vanity. Yes, I do. And my twin has been sent to punish me. I have been vain of my good looks, but I'm not vain now. My dear kind twin has seen to that. And now I loathe myself with such a loathing that I am frightened to be left alone because I want to kill myself. Doris, dear, do you know that people talk a lot of nonsense about their 'souls'? I think we can quite comfortably endure loathing our own souls, but if our bodies feel unclean we really do want to destroy them. Victor, you had better keep a very careful eye on me——"

"Nonsense, Mary. You have too much sense."

"Oh, I have got a lot more than that—I've also a twin sister who is so much more seductive to men than I can ever hope to be that they will let her take them home and murder them. Do you know, Victor, I think I am going mad. I keep on looking at my face in the mirror and wondering how it looks when I'm just about to kill——"

Wingless said: "Now listen to me, my duck. You are going to a nursing-home within the hour. And you will be in the charge of the finest doctor in the world, old Lapwing."

"And will he put me to sleep?"

"Yes, dear. Now don't you worry."

"And will he have me watched day and night, Victor, and have me kept in a locked room with iron shutters across the windows so that if I really am Jane the Ripper I shan't be able to slip out but must cut my own throat instead, which would be a very good thing, wouldn't it?"

"Mary," said Mrs. Nautigale, "stop that."

And, her eyes streaming with tears, she bent forward and kissed Mary and held her very close.

Then Wingless said: "Now that we have all let down our hair and had a good cry, I want you to help me, Mary, by trying to answer one question."

"She is in no mood," said Mrs. Nautigale, "to answer even one silly question."

"You shut up," said Wingless, "and try to look as small as you might be, dear Doris, if you didn't eat so much rich food. Now the question I want to ask you, Mary, is a rather peculiar one. Has there happened to you within the last year or so any little thing which has struck you as peculiar? Anything at all which has been outside your ordinary life? Or let me put it this way: have you met anyone at all, man or woman, or have you heard anything at all from a man or woman, which has struck you as being in any way odd?"

Mary Dove, as he spoke, had half risen on one elbow and was now staring at him with distended eyes.

"But it can't," she cried, "have anything to do with it. How can it?"

Mrs. Nautigale, breathing heavily in her excitement, bent forward and wiped off with a handkerchief a smudge of lip rouge which her kiss had left at the corner of Mary's mouth.

"Darling," she said, "then perhaps you do know something?"

"If you'll stop diving on the poor girl," Wingless snapped, "she might even be able to tell us. Well, Mary?"

"But it was just a man, George. It can't mean anything—the poor wretch. But when you asked me about anything odd that had happened—well, I suppose it *was* odd. He spoke to me on Jermyn Street."

Mary, in spite of her delicate health, usually spent the most part of the bitter month of January in London, for she was a devoted mother and would not deprive her son of the pantomimes, children's parties and Mickey Mouse festivals which are common to that season. A little after dusk on an unusually fine afternoon she was walking at her leisure up Jermyn Street, intending to rejoin her motor-car near the Ritz Hotel. She had just stopped outside Dunhill's excellent shop window and, admiring the display of improved smoking novelties within, was wishing that she too smoked so that she might possess some of those pretty things, when to her dismay she became aware that a man's face was looking at her intently over her shoulder. It was of course his reflection in the shop window that she saw, and of course she pretended to take no notice. He spoke. She walked on very quickly. Her heart was beating so, for such a thing had never before happened to her, that it was quite without her knowledge that she found herself within a narrow and elegant Arcade which seemed to her bemused senses to be entirely given up to men's haberdashery in its most refined forms.

"Madam," said a voice at her shoulder, "I must speak to you. Who are you?"

Distressed though she was, Mary could not help almost smiling at a sudden vision of herself tearing along an Arcade largely devoted to male undergarments and pursued by a man asking her who she was. The wretch must have seen the faint shadow of a smile on her profile, and been encouraged thereby, for the next thing she knew he was confronting her. She looked at him in only the most scattered way, but could not help gathering the impression that he was, in spite of his very peculiar behaviour, a presentable man.

He said: "Madam, please forgive my bad manners. It is only that I want very much to know who you are. I *must* know. You may think me mad, but I can't help it."

She said, and it sounded to her own ears extremely silly as she said it: "I don't know you. Please let me go on."

The wretch was, she now noted, of a striking sort of lean dark handsomeness. The very little she saw of his dark eyes had the queerest effect on her, as though he was trying to burn her with them.

He said: "Almost every other night for the last three years I have dreamt of you. I know every expression of your face. I know how you speak. You have become an obsession with me, Madam. Perhaps it will help me to cure this if I know who you are. Won't you help me?"

She told him her name, at which he gave no evidence of surprise whatsoever, and left him even before he had thanked her. She never saw him again, and would have forgotten all about the stupid occurrence if some three or four days later Amy had not told her that, while she and Tommy had been at a matinée one afternoon, a man had called at the house, saying he had come in connection with a benevolent fund for the distressed widowers of transatlantic airwomen. The butler had shown him into the small library downstairs, to which Amy had presently come down to him. From her description of the man's sardonically handsome looks it was obvious that it must have been the same wretch. Amy had admitted to being somewhat impressed by his looks and sincerity, and after a short interview had told him he might send the Duchess fuller particulars about the fund for which he was soliciting. But this, of course, he never did and had never intended to do, for some time after he had left it was found that he had stolen from its frame a recent photograph of Mary taken by Mr. Clarence Bray. This theft had annoyed Mary and Amy very much, since for one thing Mary was not given to indulging herself in the expense of photographs, and for another she had been so much taken by Mr. Bray's success with the likeness that she had actually ordered two copies, of which now only one remained.

And that was all. She had never seen the creature again.

"Has Amy?" Wingless asked.

Mary didn't think so. Amy was called for, and she said she hadn't. Her description of the man was not really more substantial than Mary's, except that she had at first thought the man might be a foreigner from the darkness of his complexion, and that he was about forty-five years of age.

Wingless said: "Now, Amy, Mary is going to a nursing-home for a good rest. We shall be going off within half an hour, so will you tell her maid to have the necessary things ready, and the rest can be sent along later?"

"I'll do it myself," Miss Gool said, "as Mary's maid was sent away a few days ago and we haven't yet troubled to engage another, as she goes out so seldom."

"Oh, no," Mary said, "I go out every night and have such

fun in my girlish way. Haven't you heard about it, Amy?"

At this Mrs. Nautigale's expression became so distraught that it was as though the powerful edifice of her face was being demolished with a view to structural alterations. As she dived once again on to the helpless reclining Mary, and as Miss Gool left the room, Wingless took the opportunity of doing very quickly and quietly what he thought he had to do.

Signing to Mrs. Nautigale to keep Mary occupied, his fingers searched deftly among the flimsy feminine things in her drawers and cupboards. From beneath a cloud of dainty knickers, the touch of which made him feel like a bull among ospreys, he drew out and slipped into his breast-pocket a slender blade about six inches in length curiously attached to a short handle which had been encased in rubber.

Then, kissing Mary affectionately and telling Mrs. Nautigale not to let her out of her sight until she was safely in Dr. Lapwing's charge, he left the house for Scotland Yard.

CHAPTER NINE

IN Basil Icelin's room at Scotland Yard the two men sat talking until late that night. They did not conceal from one another that they were completely flummoxed. Every now and then Superintendent Crust or a subordinate would come in with papers relating to one or other of the Jane the Ripper murders.

Colonel Wingless had detailed to the chief of the C.I.D. Mary's experience with the man in Jermyn Street and also the companion's supplementary narrative. Icelin carefully examined the blade with the curious handle, and his opinion as to the rubber covering agreed with Wingless's, that it had been glued on so as to give a better purchase for a woman's slender fingers. Wingless explained that he had searched for the knife because in a case so peculiar and evil it was wise to look for the impossible and to work backwards from the impossible to the possible.

The knife had already been examined by the chemical experts, and the gist of their report was this: the blade had been cleaned, but not expertly: in all probability it had not been used for at least six weeks to two months: a spot of dried blood extracted from between the blade and the handle belonged to the same blood-group as that of the victim of the Fulham Road Murder.

"I thought," Wingless said, "we should get some such result as that."

Icelin carefully shut the knife away in a narrow box, which would be labelled and placed among the exhibits of the Jane the Ripper crimes.

He said: "The murderess has now made two mistakes: the voice on the telephone: the knife in the Duchess's room. But these mistakes are not at all helpful to us, Wingless. Let me put it this way. They are calculated mistakes flung at our heads by a criminal who thinks she is strong enough to be able to laugh at us. There is an arrogance about them. The person who put this knife among the Duchess's whatnots did not for a moment think that I should be fool enough to believe that she knew of its existence. Now why did he or she, whatever sex this fiend is, do something which he knew would not delude the police?"

"Icelin," Wingless said, "I have come to a conclusion about that. And I am bound to tell you that this conclusion really terrifies me. Now I will give you any odds you like that within the next few days we shall find there has been a leakage to the Press and to the public about the evidence connecting the Duchess of Dove with Jane the Ripper."

Icelin said: "I'll not take an even bet on that."

"I didn't think you would. Now do you see why I say I am frightened?"

"Not quite, since you are beefy enough to prevent even the prettiest woman from cutting your throat."

Wingless said: "I can tell you jokes more amusing than that, Icelin, and one is that this criminal is not really interested in cutting throats."

"Just absent-mindedness, you mean?"

"These murders are no more than part of a plan. The false evidence against a lady of position is also an essential part of this plan. I have it in my mind, Icelin, that this criminal is not just a sex-mad ripper but someone who is trying to create an anarchy throughout this country. That is why I think there will be another murder presently, even though Mary Dove is safely under guard in a nursing-home and the police will therefore know that she cannot have committed it. And I say that after this murder there will be a leakage to the Press, and the people will be very inflamed against the police for conspiring to protect a lady of high position from arrest. Do you see, Icelin, what is in my mind? England has been greatly disturbed by factions for a year past now. If I am not wrong I think it was you yourself, as chief of the C.I.D., who warned Winston Churchill on his formation of a Coalition in the autumn of 1936 that it would be very prejudicial to the peace of this country, and that it would be considered by the increasing number of Communists as a provocative gesture, to appoint Mosley, the head of the British Union of Fascists, to the War Office."

"It's far-fetched, Wingless. Here we have a pathological criminal who murders young men after having had her pleasure with them. And from this blood-mad nymphomaniac you deduce a crazy Catiline of political conspiracy whose ambition it is to destroy the foundations of the state. You are no fool, Wingless, but I take this opportunity of saying that you sometimes speak like one."

"Don't exaggerate, Icelin—I often speak like one. But may I suggest that even from the very little that has ever penetrated into your gross mind about the mysteries of religion, it must have occurred to you that even the wisest of men doesn't know such a hell of a lot."

"Look here," Icelin said, "if you are trying to frighten me with spooks—don't, because I am a susceptible bloke and it's getting near my bedtime."

Now Basil Icelin's dark and clever eyes were serious when he said this.

"Wingless," he added, "what are you getting at?"

The big fair man across the table smiled faintly.

"I don't know. But one thing I do know is that someone or something is getting ready to give this world of ours one of the hardest kicks in the pants it's had yet."

"But what the devil," Icelin said, "has that to do with this series of unsolved and senseless murders? I don't deny what every intelligent man has known for years, that this present stage of industrial development and national expansion is nearing its end and that mankind is drifting towards a long period of world wars—which I for one hope not to see. But we are in my room at Scotland Yard, Wingless, and I am a policeman. What connection can you possibly see between our reasonable fears for the future and this sadistic murderess?"

Wingless said: "Icelin, the history of mankind is a story told in the worst possible taste and with an artistic vulgarity which would bring a blush to the cheeks of even a fashionable novelist. It is full of false melodrama, purple passages, sinister coincidences, and a sickening want of humanity. We can't deny a certain dignity to men for their resignation to the degradations piled on them by the law of creation, but I fancy a man flatters himself who sees any grandeur in the history of the human species. It's my experience that the only people who see any grandeur in the history of mankind are those who have attained leadership of some sort by trading on our worst instincts.

"But history has anyhow one quality which we must admire—its consistent co-relation of one fact with another through endless groups of facts from the beginning of time. Nothing happens which has not had a beginning in another happening. Nothing begins which has not already been begun. The seed of every event is sown by a hoary old predecessor. We cannot lift a finger which does not twitch an invisible string attached to an event in the future. That is no doubt what physicists mean when they state that the past, the present and the future are really co-existent and live together as a party of three in the house of time. And a damned uncomfortable party it is.

"Now let us descend from universal lunacies to the small backyard lunacies which have been such a help to our civilisation these last twenty years, like the Treaty of Versailles, the boycott of Russia, the collapse of the League of Nations idea, the fall of commodity prices below the cost of production, the childish malady which is still known in America as 'banking,' the peculiar default of a rather stupid man called Kreuger, then Stavisky, which led to the Paris riots of '34, the minor civil war of the year after and the re-establishment of a French Directorate last year, and now our Jane the Ripper, who is so eager to establish a family connection with an aristocratic name in a time when aristocracy is not so popular with the people as it was.

"You say this is far-fetched, Icelin, but we shall see if

you are right. I merely suggest to you that there is a strong impulse within our civilisation which is trying to hasten its destruction, and with that end in view this impulse projects a series of events—I count Kreuger and people like that as events and not as men—which act as *agents provocateurs.*"

"But all that," said Icelin, "isn't going to help us catch and hang our girl friend the Ripper."

"I," said Wingless, "I'll catch little Jane with my bow and arrow. And do you know how?"

"Neither of us does, Wingless."

"So you say. I shall start by thinking of the impossible in terms of the probable. From scratch, like a boy who believes in magic. You don't believe in magic, do you, Icelin?"

"I certainly don't believe there are fairies at the bottom of the garden."

"You mustn't be so whimsical, old chap. But isn't it odd that you don't believe in magic. For I am positive that you think a hell of a lot of science."

Icelin said: "I certainly have more confidence in Einstein than in Conan Doyle."

"The illusions created by words," Wingless said, "are really very interesting. Let me try to remember my Chesterton. A man thinks it's childish to believe in magic. But he thinks it quite grown-up to believe in mathematics. He thinks it idiotic to believe in miracles. But he worships Marconi. I see I shall have to appeal to your material side, Icelin. Now do you see any connection between these peculiar Jane the Ripper crimes and science?"

"My God," said Icelin, "I believe I've got what you are driving at." He called sharply into the buzzer, and Superintendent Crust came in, and he said: "This is urgent, Crust. I want you to take charge personally, for it needs great delicacy. I fancy we have no authority whatsoever to question the General Medical Council. You had better put it that the Secretary of the Council will be doing us a great favour if he gives us a list of the names and addresses of all doctors——"

"And surgeons," said Wingless.

"—who have either been censured or barred from practising by the General Medical Council since, let us say, 1920."

"There should be no difficulty about that, sir."

Icelin glanced at Wingless. "Anything to suggest?"

"Yes, but I don't think it's possible. Photographs of these blokes would be helpful, but I don't suppose the G.M.C. keeps a portrait gallery."

"Sir," said Crust, "there will be no difficulty about getting the names. But it won't be easy tracing them to where they are living now. And it's only by tracing them we can get photographs, if then."

"Why should it be so difficult, Crust?"

"Sir, barred doctors are usually described as 'of no occupation.' And it's easiest to trace a man by his occupation."

Icelin said: "Go ahead, anyway. You have got only this to go on—our man can't be more than fifty and maybe lives in London."

As Crust went out Icelin glanced at his watch and yawned. It was just eleven o'clock. A long day's work.

Wingless said: "What about walking with me to my club for a drink? I've got a feeling that there is something odd going on in London to-night and that we might see something of it."

But Icelin was tired, and when they went out into Whitehall he hailed a taxi and said good-night.

CHAPTER TEN

WINGLESS, having passed through the crowd emerging from the Whitehall Theatre at the close of the performance, hesitated at the corner of Trafalgar Square. Should he walk through Admiralty Arch and up the Mall, or should he engage himself against fearful odds by crossing Trafalgar Square towards the National Gallery? The spiteful narrow mouth of the Strand, which captains the noisy cohorts of the W.C.2 district and is always ready to inconvenience its betters, the spacious squares and wide avenues of S.W.1 and W.1, was discharging against its enemies a roar of buses, a flight of taxis and a pride of limousines. Cockspur Street across Trafalgar Square received these missiles with the sullen dignity of the defenceless, for being a one-way street she got all the kicks and none of the fun. Wingless, bending at both knees and clutching his stick firmly as a support, tottered forth into the maelstrom in the guise of a cripple and, amid a howl of outraged brakes, but with the bored encouragement of a policeman, threaded his way across so slowly that the sympathy of bus drivers for the halt and the blind was put to a very severe strain.

This tomfoolery, which was doing his depression a world of good, came to an end when he caught sight of a small crowd by one of the lions on the National Gallery side of the Column. There were about fifteen people, all men but one, being addressed by a pot-bellied little man in an indignant voice of great carrying power. They looked the usual group of nondescripts who collect around speakers in some of London's open spaces, and would not have attracted Wingless's attention had he not heard above the roar of the traffic the words "Jane the Ripper."

As he approached he noticed that the crowd was thickening quickly around the pot-bellied little speaker. They were a sullen-looking lot, on the whole. There was no "friendly backchat" or "unfailing sense of humour" about them. Two policemen stood nearby with expressions of remote disinterestedness. Wingless did not trouble to push his way to the front of the crowd, for the oratorical arts of the little speaker did not include that of cultured restraint.

"Why?" he was shouting. "Why? That's wot every mother's son of us all is arsking ourselves. Friends, the conscience of the people grinds slowly—but when it starts grinding, friends, it grinds like 'ell and without fear or favour to rich and poor or 'igh and low. The righteous anger of the people is a fearful thing—but, friends, it is the people's right to be angry against injustice and clarss prejudice. I say it again—CLARSS PREJUDICE."

"Here," said one of the policemen, with that scholarly intonation with which London has grown resentfully familiar since the long and memorable administration of Lord Trenchard as Commissioner. "Here, try speaking a bit lower, will you?"

"The voice of justice," hissed the little man indignantly, "doesn't 'ave to shout to be 'eard. Now, friends, I am going to arsk you a plain question: WHY 'asn't this Jane the Ripper been cort? Why 'asn't this fiend in yewman form been 'ung by the neck until she is dead? Friends, that's wot the voice of the people is arsking. Why 'asn't this vampire been arrested? I'll TELL you why, friends. And I'll tell you in one word—clarss. Did you 'ear me? I said—clarss. That's why the Ripper 'asn't been arrested yet—and that's why she won't ever be arrested—because England is 'idebound by clarss prejudice and the police is 'idebound by clarss prejudice—and, friends, we're blamed fools to stand it. Wot would 'ave happened to the Ripper if she 'ad been a working woman gone nuts? She'd 'ave been strung up long since. But, friends, she 'asn't even been arrested—and for why? Because she's a ruddy marchioness or a lousy duchess with a great name but narsty 'abits——"

Wingless went over to the two young policemen, told them he was a friend of Mr. Icelin, and suggested that one of them should run the few hundred yards to Scotland Yard to fetch Superintendent Crust. He added that the matter was urgent and had to do with investigations which the Superintendent was making. When, rather doubtfully, one of the policemen had gone off at a good pace, Wingless said to the other: "Can't we hold that little chap on anything?"

The young policeman, an Old Malvernian who had recently passed into the force with honours in Literature and Classical History from the Trenchard Police College, said: "I daresay we might, sir, if it was worth it. But it so seldom is. It's usually better to let them dither away."

The pot-bellied little man had evidently come to the end of his exhortations, and the crowd was moving away. They were a quiet lot, mostly men, but Wingless again noticed that there was about them a sullen look unusual in the ordinary English crowd. The pot-bellied little man was left talking to three men in a low voice, glancing occasionally in the policeman's direction.

Wingless said: "My advice to you, constable, is not to let our little friend go before Mr. Crust comes."

"There's no difficulty, sir, about holding him for a bit on a charge of inciting to violence. I'll keep an eye on him until the Superintendent gets here."

At that moment Crust was seen approaching them,

walking with surprising swiftness for a man of his bulk. Wingless quickly explained why it might be worth their while to put a few questions to the antagonist of "clarss." Then Crust went up to the little man, from whom his companions instantly melted away, and said gloomily: "Come on, Joe. Just want to ask you a few questions."

"Me?" said the little man indignantly. "Wot should I come along for?" But at the same time he winked with surprising amiability at Wingless, as though to say he was the last man in the world to prevent a superintendent from having his little joke.

When they were in Crust's room at Scotland Yard, the Superintendent said: "Now we are not charging you with anything, Joe Chundle. Anyway, not if you behave yourself. But do you realise you are laying yourself open to the charge of uttering seditious speeches? Your usual line is speaking on atheism. What has made you change to Jane the Ripper?"

"My conscience," said Joe, with the resigned air of a man not unused to having his word doubted.

"Now, Joe, don't come that over me. I've known you too long. I want two answers to two questions, and I want them quick. Who put you on to this Jane the Ripper lay? And who told you to spread around this daft story about her being a lady of title?"

Mr. Chundle said: "Look 'ere, Super, this is getting too deep for me. I'll tell you all I know, but it ain't anything. I can't tell you who's spreading the rumour because I don't know, but you could 'ear it in every pub to-night before closing. The chap who told me about it didn't know more'n I did, but he gave me five bob to do my bit about Jane the Ripper and say she was being protected because of 'er position. Lord bless me, Super, there must have been 'undreds of chaps like me that was . . ."

The telephone bell rang. The Superintendent listened without a word for quite three minutes. As he slowly replaced the receiver, he said absently: "All right, Joe. But mind you stick to atheism in future. It's more respectable."

When they were alone he got up and took up his bowler, and then stood staring into it. His great clumsy figure sagged at the shoulders as though he had suddenly given way to an overwhelming fatigue. There was a strained look in his melancholy eyes as he turned to Wingless.

"Sir," he said, "maybe I ought to ring up Mr. Icelin at his home, but I just haven't the heart. He has been in his office here since eight this morning working his head off, and a man must get some rest some time. You can come along with me if you like, sir. This news is going to shake London a bit too much for my liking."

"What is it, Crust?"

"Sir," said Crust, "the Inspector at Vine Street has just reported that the decapitated head of a man was found fifteen minutes ago just inside the railings of the Green Park almost opposite Half Moon Street. It was in a white cardboard hat-box. The Green Park is closed now, and the hat-box must have been chucked over the top of the railings, because the lid had fallen off. The woman who first saw through the railings what was in the box had a fit, and no wonder."

"You're right," Wingless said, as they drove northwards in the police car. "This is going to shake things up quite a bit."

The Superintendent looked at him with a very mournful expression.

"Sir," said he, "but that's not all, nor the worst of it. A perfumed card was found pinned to the poor chap's forehead, and the perfume is quite unmistakable."

"Nothing written on the card?"

"Didn't I tell you, sir? 'Isn't it a ripping day? With

cordial good wishes from Jane the Ripper.' I'd like," said the Superintendent, "to wring the bitch's neck for her impudence."

"Man," said Wingless, "do you call a severed head no more than impudence?"

"Sir," said Crust, "maybe I'm going goofy myself. Did I forget to tell you that the constable who examined the head found that it was a wax head, very lifelike to be sure, and that the blood, of which there was naturally a large amount, was some kind of coloured chemical."

"I'll be darned," said Wingless.

"And me," said the Superintendent. "But what does get my goat is that this severed wax head is maybe going to cause more trouble than the three murders put together. And do you know why, sir? Because the public is in no mood to believe what the police tell them, and so the public won't believe it wasn't a real head. And, sir," said old Crust, looking gloomily into his bowler hat, "if I'm not right I'll eat this hat."

CHAPTER ELEVEN

THE July Riots in London must make that year for ever infamous in the glorious history of England. To our enlightened civilisation, hitherto founded on the Credit System—which means that the rich man owes his duty to God and the poor man owes his to God-knows-who—the Riots were a shocking revelation of the corrupt passions that are born of over-education. Two Commissions of Enquiry are still deliberating upon the causes, aspects and suppression of the disorders, and much reliance is placed upon their findings. But it would appear that they are suffering a good deal of discomfort, for a Commission's dilemma is grave which must combine severity with sagacity and temper justice with compromise. You know how it is when whatever you do is wrong anyway.

These admirable Commissions have issued certain pronouncements. For example, Lord Buick of Barstow, always a safe man to rebuke, has been rebuked for having permitted his newspapers to publish during the Riots statements of a kind likely to inflame and misdirect the more unthinking amongst the populace. The Viscounts Astor and Rothermere, the Barons Beaverbrook and Camrose, and of course their eldest sons, have on the other hand been commended for their sane and sound attitude of praising the restraint of the rioters, the restraint of the police, the restraint of the Fascists, and the restraint of everyone concerned, except of course of a handful of foreign agitators, on whom they very properly put the blame: Lord Beaverbrook adding a rider to the effect that such things could not happen in England if we bought less beef from the Argentine and made more butter in England.

The scholars of Eton College had also emerged with credit from the Enquiry, as was only to be expected. These brave lads had no sooner heard that revolution was threatening the capital than they marched on London. They must have been stopped by the surprised policemen on the way had they not represented themselves, quite correctly, as a march of the unemployed. They were unarmed, except with such blunt instruments as they could pick up on the way. Marching up from Knightsbridge they attacked the rioters with peculiar fitness at Hyde Park Corner, beneath the gaze of the iron Duke of Wellington who, permitting himself to overlook the geographical claims of Belgian soil, had said that Waterloo was won near Windsor.

The Commission of Enquiry recorded with admiration an

incident of the Battle of Hyde Park Corner. In the very heat of the engagement, when the brave lads had just stormed the Communists' barricades stretching from Wellington's statue to the gates of the Park, it was noticed that an elderly nurse wheeling a pram was waiting at the corner of Constitution Hill to cross to the Park. Instantly a truce was declared and the nurse and her charge, escorted by one Etonian with a bleeding nose and one Communist with a black eye, were allowed to proceed between the silent ranks of the combatants into the Park.

It was to this incident, which reflected great credit on all concerned, that the schoolboys put down their ultimate defeat just before lunch-time. For these brave lads, hitherto supported only by thoughts of protecting England's great traditions against the ignoble changes of a revolution, were reminded by the baby in the pram of their own not very distant childhood and of their still less distant parents, and their enthusiasm was somewhat damped by doubts as to the recognition which their services to the State would receive from their mothers. However, they retreated in good order just before lunch-time, leaving the field to the Communists, who had wisely brought their luncheons with them in the form of sausage rolls and a tasty bit of pork pie here and there, no doubt supplied to them by alien agitators.

They were shortly to regret the effect of this rich nourishment on their powers of endurance. For the Corps of Commissionaires, leaving for the time the patrons of exclusive hotels to find their own taxis, flushed with indignation, ablaze with medals honourably won on the field of battle, and undeterred by thoughts of their mothers, who had anyhow not had the forethought to send them to public schools, marched up Piccadilly and speedily demolished the pretensions of the Communists.

We must not forget to add that the conduct of the police throughout the rioting was warmly approved by the Commission. They had been told neither to provoke the Communists in any way nor to seem to side with the Fascists. Their restraint in these particulars was admirable, and their discretion called for the highest praise. But they stood no nonsense and put down rowdyism with a firm hand. When Hyde Park Corner had been cleared of fighters and the shopkeepers in the neighbourhood had come to have a look at the mess, the police instantly charged them with drawn truncheons and arrested several for loitering.

The Riots began with sporadic rowdyism on the morning after the finding of the severed head in the Green Park, which nobody believed was made of wax, and lasted for three days. The rioters' first objective was the Duchess of Dove's house in Grosvenor Square. Exactly how the suspicions of these wretches had become fixed on the gentle Duchess will probably always remain a mystery. What is certain is that great numbers of the more violent sort, convinced that Jane the Ripper was being protected by the authorities merely because she was the Duchess of Dove, had determined to take the law into their own hands. They called loudly for justice. They screamed their abhorrence of favouritism. They spat on privilege. They proclaimed Lynch Law.

Storming Grosvenor Square in two columns of approximately a thousand persons each, one pouring down Bruton Street and one down South Audley Street from the north, these wretches had Mayfair at their mercy. The police, taken by surprise, and forewarned only of probable attacks on the House of Commons through the day, sought in vain to keep them from their objective. With little difficulty the more arrogant amongst the mob forced their way into the Duchess's house, having previously smashed every window in the

Square to the strains of the *Internationale,* which they sang with an accuracy possible only to those who had been suborned and trained by alien agitators.

Once within the Duchess's house the rioters, amongst whom it is regrettable to report that there were as many women as men, smashed everything they could see with the most disagreeable thoroughness imaginable. Nor did they behave in any way with that good-humoured restraint which it has always been our pride to discern in the behaviour of the English crowd as compared with crowds abroad, who have not of course been taught the principles of fair play. It is with distaste we learn that they did not respect even the privacy of the Duchess's bedroom, and that her daintily-appointed bathroom and privy appeared especially to infuriate the women among the mob.

Had Mary Dove been in her room her fate must have been horrible, for several of the men were so lost to all human feelings that they had come prepared with ropes with which to hang her out of the window in the sight of their gratified friends below. Nor were the women backward in suggesting the most vile humiliations that might be put upon her body. They had to content themselves with lesser outrages. And, unable to destroy the object of their primitive anger, they wreaked their vengeance on her property by hurling everything they could lay hands on out of the broken windows to the yelling crowd below.

Thus the charming but private details of a gentlewoman's bedchamber became the derided objects of the rioters' lust, and the coarse hands of the mob delighted to destroy the flimsy fabrics of a duchess's intimate toilet. While London, on that wretched day, was not spared the degrading spectacle of Englishmen wearing in broad daylight a lady's knickers as fancy headgear.

But worse was yet to come. The crowd in the Square became so inflamed by the revelation of what the rich wore next to their pampered skins while the unemployment figures went up—or down, what the hell?—every week, that they began storming the other houses in the Square and debauching their contents. So that presently when a column of Fascists marched into Grosvenor Square from Carlos Place they were met by the disgusting spectacle of common men and women wearing on their heads the chamber-pots of some of the proudest families in England.

But before the Fascists appeared to distract the attention of the rioters, Miss Gool had suffered a great deal. Those depraved wretches would not believe that the Duchess was not concealed within the house. They would not believe that she had escaped their vengeance. They therefore subjected Miss Gool to every form of insult, though her repeated statements before the Commission of Enquiry that she had been made the object of abominable lusts were unanimously denied by those rioters who were later arrested and who protested most vehemently that Miss Gool was not at all their idea of a nice bit of skirt.

The temper of the rebels in the neighbourhood of Westminster was less licentious but more dangerous. Here the foul features of revolution were clearly to be seen. The mob's objective was nothing less than the seat of Government, and the hostility of the people was directed with bitter tenacity at the inviolable persons of their elected representatives. It is not known whether they also contemplated the awful crime of high treason against the Crown, but it is odds on that they did. To these dangerous revolutionaries the affair of the Duchess of Dove was no more than an excuse for carrying out an anarchy they had long contemplated. Falsely representing their ambitions to the deluded people to be the setting up of a Republic, they sought to destroy by violence the Constitution of England and to erect in its place a shameful tyranny.

It was only through the reluctance of the Cabinet to call out armed troops, and thus dignify a riot by treating it as a rebellion and expose to a critical world the proud civilisation of England at last scarred by Civil War, that the disorders could have lasted so long as they did. Nor was London, on the second and most furious night of the rioting, spared the furious agonies of revolution. And even the most depraved of the Communists were abashed, even the most besotted of the rioters sought the obscurity of their homes, when the cry of "Fire!" was raised and a pillar of smoke was seen to mount with awful solemnity from the direction of Whitehall.

It can be imagined with what relief the people of London, who retain even under the utmost stress a sense of proportion, and would have been very properly horrified at the burning of an Underground station or a public lavatory, learnt that the fire had destroyed nothing more important than some paintings in a wing of the Tate Gallery. This could have been the work only of alien agitators ignorant of the Englishman's sterling good sense, whereas of course a native agitator would have destroyed the pitch at the Oval, where a somewhat quarrelsome cricket-match with Australia was at that time being played.

It should be explained that amongst the informed the innocence of Mary Dove was never in doubt, and that the esteem in which she was always held became touched with reverence for a lady so unfairly persecuted. Safe in Dr. Lapwing's care, poor Mary heard only the distant echoes of the rioting and knew nothing either of the crazy destruction of her home or of the vindictiveness of the mob against her person.

The rioting had no sooner been suppressed than Scotland

Yard was subjected both in the House of Commons and the Press to the most severe criticism for not having yet caught the fiend known as Jane the Ripper. The temporary Commissioner of Police, glad of the excuse, instantly resigned and retired to public life, for which his social ambitions and his wife's toothy tenacity eminently fitted him. In the absence of anyone ready to take on the job at so critical a time, Basil Icelin became Acting Commissioner.

Throughout the days of the rioting neither the C.I.D. nor our friend Colonel Wingless had been idle in their quest of the criminal. And, some few mornings after the last of the disorders, there took place what at first appeared to be a singular coincidence.

CHAPTER TWELVE

Towards noon Wingless was driving his car through the main street of Leatherhead when he saw Icelin and Superintendent Crust in conversation on the pavement with a uniformed Police Sergeant. Icelin raised an eyebrow as his friend drew up.

"And what are you doing here, Wingless?"

"I shouldn't wonder," Wingless said, "if we haven't by some extraordinary fluke hit on the same trail."

"Sir," said Superintendent Crust, "we at Scotland Yard can't afford to make flukes. We are here as a result of certain investigations, and with Mr. Icelin's permission, sir, I could tell you their nature."

"By all means," Icelin said, "since it was you who first gave us the line to take, Wingless. But if you are here after the same man, I'm damned if I know how you managed to get on to him."

"All this," said Wingless, "calls for a quick one." Whereupon the three men entered an inn nearby, the Sergeant promising to attend on them in half an hour's time.

"Sir," said Superintendent Crust, looking mournfully into a tankard of ale, "I must tell you first of all that the Secretary of the General Medical Council gave us every assistance in his power, and that as a result of his collaboration we are here to find out all we can about a man called Axaloe. Now this man Axaloe, sir, was a doctor and scientist of exceptional achievements, but what was remarkable about him was that he was also very interested in spiritualism."

"And why was that remarkable, Crust?"

"Sir, a mind so exact as this man Axaloe's must naturally abhor the daft delusions and barmy theories on which occult data are based. And if I seem to express myself too strongly about this, it is because my wife's sister, sir, is very partial to spiritualism——"

"And has she tried, Crust, to convert you?"

"Sir, to an unhinged mind like my wife's sister's everything appears possible. Now, some twelve years ago the General Medical Council found itself compelled to investigate certain alleged irregularities in this Dr. Xanthis Axaloe's professional conduct. These irregularities, which were proved against him without difficulty and for which he was debarred from earning his livelihood as a doctor, were of a singularly unpleasant nature. The husbands of two of Dr. Axaloe's lady patients indignantly complained that their wives returned home after a consultation in an exhausted, nervous and hysterical condition quite incompatible with a visit to a respectable physician. Sir," said Superintendent Crust, "I shall not go into the details of the offences which this man had committed upon the minds and persons of these unfortunate ladies—who, to the proper indignation of their husbands, refused to testify against him—except to tell you that he was proved beyond all doubt to be a man more gross and more depraved than any other man you ever heard of."

"What were these offences, Crust?"

"Sir, I would not sully your ears."

"You do an injustice to the Colonel's clubs," said Icelin. "His ears have been sullied by experts."

"The man," said Crust indignantly, "was a sapphist and a nymphomaniac."

"Must be an acrobat," said Wingless.

"He means," said Icelin, "sadist and erotomaniac."

"Sir," said Crust warmly, "that's as may be, but this man Axaloe was a downright shocking chap, that's what he was. You never heard of such goings on, and what those poor ladies must have suffered—or should have suffered if they had been brought up right—doesn't bear thinking of. There were police court proceedings and Axaloe was committed to hard labour for eighteen months. Now, sir, his photograph is conclusive evidence that he was the man who addressed her Grace in Jermyn Street and later had the audacity to call at her house.

"The report of the Governor of the prison in which he served his sentence is very interesting. The convict Axaloe, while his conduct throughout was of a kind to earn him the usual remission, remained until his release the most hated and the most feared inmate of the prison amongst both warders and convicts. The Governor could find no definite reason for this fear and hatred, but could only suggest that it must have been due to the very dark, icy and contemptuous stare with which this man Axaloe made for himself a prison within the prison walls. But the Governor dismissed as superstitious nonsense certain remarks in a very popular book recently published by an ex-convict who had served his sentence with

Axaloe, to the effect that Xanthis Axaloe—under another name in the book, of course—was an Antichrist with great and virulent powers. Sir," said Superintendent Crust, "the fact remains that we have at this stage nothing tangible with which to connect this man Axaloe with the Jane the Ripper crimes."

"Then let me ask you," said Wingless, "how it comes about that I also have come to Leatherhead for a little chat with Dr. Axaloe?"

"Perhaps," said Icelin, "you consulted Crust's wife's sister."

"If he had, sir," said poor Crust, "he would still be listening to her."

"Only four days ago," Wingless said, "a point occurred to me which I had quite overlooked——"

"But we hadn't," said Icelin. "You are referring to the Duchess's maid, Monica Snee, who was dismissed by Miss Gool some six weeks ago. She has been traced and interviewed, Wingless. Her character in the neighbourhood where she lives is excellent, she had seen nothing while in service at Grosvenor Square of a suspicious nature, she expressed respectful affection for her former mistress and an understandable resentment against Miss Gool—and, in short, my dear fellow, she was a wash-out."

"You surprise me," said Wingless, "but not half as much as little Monica did. My valet and I have been taking it in turns to follow her day and night for several days, and we have also searched her rooms in Camberwell."

"An illegal act," said Icelin. "We also found nothing."

"Exactly. But yesterday afternoon, Crust, my man followed her into a train at Waterloo. She got out here at Leatherhead and walked to a cottage beyond the town, where she stayed for several hours. My man found that this cottage had been owned for some years by a recluse called Champion, who went out very rarely and then only at night, was of presentable appearance, and was understood to be interested in some form of research."

"Sir," said Superintendent Crust, "I take the liberty of asking you to have one on me. You have done very well, sir, very well indeed. You have brought home the bacon, Colonel Wingless."

"You think it is the same man, Crust?"

"I have already ascertained, sir, that Xanthis Axaloe is passing under the name of Percy Champion. Now, thanks to what you have told us, maybe we shall get him yet. And when we do, sir, only my long training as a police officer will prevent me from twisting his dratted neck—if you will pardon me, sir—with my own hands."

Icelin said: "You are too optimistic, Crust. As you said before, we haven't one thing against Axaloe in the Jane case. And *how*, in the name of all reason, can he be Jane?"

"Sir, this is a very queer case."

"Are you telling me, Crust? You have suggested that we interview him. May I ask what we can—legally—do if he refuses to be interviewed?"

At this Superintendent Crust looked more than usually despondent, for Icelin's question had been worrying him for the last twenty-four hours. Colonel Wingless wore a faraway look, but it was impossible to say whether that was due to a plan he had or to the gins-and-bitters he had been drinking.

After a luncheon of those damp cold meats for which England is renowned or infamous according to the lining of your stomach, the three men left the inn and were joined by the Sergeant, who had been patiently waiting for them. Drawn up in front of Wingless's open car there was an Austin saloon with a beefy-looking man in a bowler hat at the wheel.

"Is that," Icelin said severely to the Sergeant, "a plain-clothes man?"

"Yes, sir."

"Then tell him," said Crust, "to go away at once."

"Leaving the car behind, sir?"

"No, no—I want him away as quickly as may be. Why, I never heard of such a thing. All Leatherhead will be taking us for gangsters in a jiffy."

Then Crust turned to Icelin. "We haven't one tittle of authority, sir. This man Axaloe can send us to the dickens or not just as he chooses. Or he can 'phone his lawyer. Or, worse still, a newspaper editor. Now I suggest we drive in the Colonel's car near the house—the Sergeant will show us the way—and you and Colonel Wingless can call on him as private individuals."

"And what," said Wingless, "do we do then? Just ask him his views on birth control and if he doesn't answer with charm tell him he's a bastard?"

"Just tell him, sir, that you are Monica Snee's uncle and guardian and ask him why a gent like him is compromising the poor girl. All we want, sir, is to get you two gentlemen into the house and keep him occupied while I get in at the back and search the place. He keeps no servants, I'm told by the Sergeant here, just because no one will stay with him. If he's offhand with you, sir," said Crust to Wingless, "just clip him one good and hard."

"Would you advise the jaw, Crust, or lower down?"

"The jaw should do very nicely, sir. It's an illegal assault, of course, but I don't fancy Axaloe will make any charge. He might 'phone his lawyer when he has recovered, but I'll have searched the place by then. And, sir, giving him this alleged sock on the jaw will not only be a refreshment to you but a great help to the police, so make it extra special."

"I shall try, Crust, to deserve your confidence."

But perhaps Colonel Wingless had lost something of his old swiftness. Perhaps the bottle, that enemy of the human species, particularly when taken regularly between meals, had corrupted his vitality. For Xanthis Axaloe smote him, and he fell to the ground.

Now the house which the Sergeant pointed out to them, when Wingless had stopped the car some distance away, looked a most unsuitable residence for a man of Dr. Axaloe's sinister reputation. The surroundings were tranquil and charming, and the ripe scents of high summer were heavy in the air. Icelin and Wingless felt their town clothes a burden on them as, leaving Crust and the Sergeant by the car, they walked down the lane. High hedges screened them from the house until they were abreast. The place was as bright as a new pin, very white, and the shutters newly painted green.

"I've got an aunt," said Wingless, "who has a place the sister of this."

"To hell with your aunt," said Icelin.

"Right, old chap. I'll tell her."

"Wingless, I like this business less and less. There is something about this man that gives me a queasy feeling in the belly. Got a gun with you?"

"Funny you should ask that. I was just thinking that the best way to interview this bloke would be to shoot him first."

Throughout this interchange they were partly screened from the house by the hedge. Wingless strode to the garden gate, threw it open and, followed by Icelin, marched up the narrow path to the green door. There was a brass knocker and a bell button.

"All together," said Wingless. "I knock and you ring."

"But why knock?"

"Because I shall feel a lot better after having made a noise. Now."

The noise he made with the heavy brass knocker was so very considerable, and the silence that followed so very depressing, that he almost immediately knocked again.

"Feel better?" said Icelin sourly.

At that moment the door was opened, and the two men were so surprised by what they saw that they gaped. For the dark, lean, hairy and handsome man before them was wearing a salmon-pink bathing-costume of a very tight, very modish and decidedly feminine cut. Two dainty straps supported it over the man's powerful shoulders, and it was cut away at each side to give a splendid if unexpected view of his ribs. What the back was like, they could only imagine. And this salmon-pink frippery, incongruous though it must have been on any man, was fantastic on the one before them, for his tall and sinewy figure, his manly parts, his dark narrow handsome features and the icy smile in his deep eyes, were of a pronouncedly masculine order.

"Mr. Axaloe?" said Wingless.

"*Ci-devant*," said the man. "Now Champion."

"We want," said Icelin, "to ask you some questions with reference to your alleged intimacy with a Monica Snee."

"Why 'alleged'?" said the man coldly. "I have been sleeping with her off and on for months. What about it?"

Nonplussed by this Gallic statement of fact in a matter where insinuation is usually held to be the gentleman's part, particularly if, like Icelin, he belongs to a really good club, Icelin looked doubtfully at Wingless.

"Not a nice man," said Wingless.

"Nice?" said Icelin. "He must be a terror with the girls."

"Sir," said Wingless to the man, "I am surprised at your speaking in such terms of a respectable girl."

"I don't give a curse," said the man, "whether you are surprised or not. And Monica Snee isn't a respectable girl. She can take it."

"It?" said Icelin.

"The girl's a tart," said the man.

"Now don't get cross," said Wingless.

"Why not?" said the man. "Wouldn't you be if your girl had played ball with almost every manservant in Grosvenor Square?"

"Look here," said Wingless with a severity he was far from feeling, for he himself had once had an eye for pretty Monica but had been deceived by her prim expression, "look here, I am here on the girl's behalf. Let me tell you, Dr. Axaloe or Mr. Champion or whoever you are, that I am the girl's uncle and——"

"Colonel Wingless," said the man in the bathing-costume, "you are a damned liar."

Throughout this conversation the man Axaloe had been standing a yard or so within the doorway. Wingless, who was a good half-head the taller of the two, had managed to edge himself just into the narrow passage, while Icelin had moved a little to one side to give his friend elbow-room for the arranged blow. Now, as the word "liar" cracked across his hearing, Icelin braced himself to push into the house after Wingless. Thus he was unprepared for the impact of a moving body in a contrary direction, and when Wingless was forced back on him as though he had been hit by a ton of bricks the two men fell ignominiously into a flower bed. The door was closed.

"Damn it," said Icelin, "can't you get off my ankle?"

Wingless, tenderly feeling his jaw-bone, got up with a dazed expression.

"Believe it or not," he said.

Then, very thoughtfully, he walked out of the garden, and Icelin followed him.

Wingless said: "What struck you—now, no jokes—as most odd about our friend?"

Icelin said: "The bathing-costume."

"But a bathing-costume on a hot day isn't in itself very odd."

"No. But it isn't every man of forty or so who wears a salmon-pink bathing-costume made for a young lady of fashion."

"That's just what I think."

"This business," said Icelin, "is monkey business."

"And do you know, Icelin, I am going back to that house to see exactly how queer it is."

"Without going into training first?"

"We'll engage in badinage later, shall we?"

"I'm sorry, old man. But this Jane the Ripper case has gotten on my nerves. Now let me tell you that if you go back to that house the police can't really keep an eye on you. Crust and I can watch out as private citizens. We have nothing against this man. The fact that he served a sentence more than twelve years ago lays him open to suspicion. But that's all. I tell you frankly, Wingless, that the police can't afford to antagonise public feeling any further at the moment. Any action against this man which isn't based on absolute facts must lay us open to the charge of persecuting the individual."

They were now back beside Wingless's car. Crust and the Sergeant were not to be seen.

Wingless said: "I gather from that that you are with me in whatever I do."

Icelin's lean clever face was very pale.

"Yes, but not as a policeman. I don't think I'm a coward, Wingless. But I am frightened of this man."

Wingless said: "So am I. I'm so darned scared that the muscles of my legs are getting strained from trying to keep my knees steady. And my family is liable to varicose veins, too."

Crust appeared through a gap in the hedge, followed by the Sergeant. Wingless gave him a vague grin and started pacing up and down the lane with his hands deep in his pockets. Icelin told Crust what had happened.

"Sir," Crust said, "we have made one hell of a mistake. We have warned our man before having anything against him. What we should have done, sir, and what we must do now, is to get to London as quickly as may be and take a good long look at the girl Monica Snee. Colonel Wingless, sir," said Crust, "did you hear what I said?"

"I heard you, Crust. Take my car. Mr. Icelin can drive it, or thinks he can. If he can't, sell it and hire a taxi."

"You are not coming with us, sir?"

"Did I never tell you, Crust, that I am a horticulturist?"

"Sir," said Crust, "it had slipped my mind. So it is your intention to stay here and while away a few hours by looking at the pretty flowers in the neighbourhood?"

"You have exactly guessed my mind, Crust."

Icelin, with a sidelong look at the Superintendent, who nodded, said: "It's close on half-past three now. We'll come back for you about six."

Wingless said: "Not much later, please. It's apt to get damp in the evenings."

"Sir," said Crust, "while I am not a horticulturist myself I have ascertained that there is what you might call a certain technique about it. Am I wrong, sir, in thinking that a tall man is apt to stoop to look at a flower?"

"You are right, Crust."

"Then, sir, there is a chance that he might be caught in a position which is commonly known as 'bending'."

"I gather," said Wingless, pocketing the revolver which Crust gave him, "that this is not merely a Scotland Yard exhibit but is loaded with the usual conveniences?"

"You bet it is," said Crust. "Therefore, sir, you must exercise great care in not aiming it in any given direction."

"But suppose it goes off by accident?"

"And aren't I supposing just that?" said Superintendent Crust.

CHAPTER THIRTEEN

We have now to relate the true history of the inexplicable events that took place in the course of that summer afternoon within the white house not far from Leatherhead.

Icelin and Superintendent Crust had never, of course, any intention of permitting Colonel Wingless to carry on the burden of the investigation alone. Therefore Icelin wrote a note to the Chief Constable of the county, who was fortunately a friend and admirer of his, and gave it to the Sergeant to take back to Leatherhead. Then, when no more than ten minutes had elapsed since Wingless had left them, the two men slipped through the gap in the hedge and made for their objective across the fields.

There was very little cover for them as they approached the white house from the back, but it seemed unlikely that the man Axaloe would spot them, as he must be interviewing Wingless at the front. And that Wingless had this time effected an entrance seemed certain, since there was no sign of him. The garden, or rather field, at the back of Axaloe's house was very easily accessible once they had crossed a railway embankment, but before approaching the back entrance the two men stood thoughtfully looking at the quiet scene before them.

"It's uncommonly quiet," said Icelin.

"Sir, I'll tell you why. There's no dog."

"But that doesn't make sense. What sort of a man would it be, Crust, who can live alone in the country without a dog?"

"So help me God," said Crust, "I'll never sleep easy again until we find out."

They made for the back of the house, but when they gently tried to open a door that was there and a window giving into a tidy kitchen they found the one locked and the other bolted. Hugging the wall, one behind the other, they then made for the front, where the pretty wild garden was a bright contrast to the desolate scene they had left. Crouching, so that they should not be seen from the windows, they cautiously went forward towards the front door in the hope that Axaloe had left it open or unlatched. But they did not reach the door. They were held, they were frozen, by Wingless's voice, which came to them very clearly from the open window immediately above their stooping heads.

"No," Wingless said, "I won't have any tea. But do you think there's such a thing as a whisky-and-soda in this house, Mary?"

Then the two crouching men stared at one another.

"Well," Crust whispered, "this surely beats cock-fighting."

"But how," said Icelin, gulping down the nausea which kept rising within him, "but how could she have got here without our seeing her? Could she have been here with Axaloe since before we came?"

"Sir, the question is how could the Duchess have got away from the nursing-home, this morning it must have been, without Colonel Wingless or the police having been notified at once?"

Since the first shock of Wingless's voice from the window above their heads they had heard no other words but only the rattle of a cup, maybe, and the creak of a chair. Crust and Icelin, still crouching, backed out of the line of vision before straightening out their cramped knees. And then they saw Wingless standing at the open window, his great body filling it. And he was looking straight at them, as though he had known of their presence all the time.

He said: "Mary is here, Icelin."

Now Icelin was very white, but Wingless's ruddy face was as blanched as though the devil had kissed him on the mouth.

"Sir," said Crust, "then we must do our duty."

Wingless said: "Go ahead."

Crust said: "I have a warrant here in my pocket, made out three weeks ago but not used before owing to the peculiar circumstances you know of. But now, sir, we can no longer avoid the necessity of immediately arresting Mary Wingless St. Cloud Bull, Duchess of Dove, for murder."

Icelin and Crust had now approached the open window. Their heads came to about Wingless's middle within the room, which was furnished comfortably as a parlour and library. On an easy chair well within the room, her calm and lovely profile turned to them in the act of sipping from a cup of tea, sat the gracious young woman whom they knew to be the Duchess of Dove. Her clustered curly hair was free from any covering, and her arms were bare, for she was loosely dressed in white as a woman might be in her own house who is receiving only intimate friends. Her expression was so serene and unconcerned that Icelin had literally to pinch himself to realise that here was a woman with a rope around her slender neck. But Crust, looking sombrely at her, could think only of what a matchless actress this murderess must be, for with her diffidence and her blushing and her sensitive modesty she had quite taken him in when he had called on her that morning in Grosvenor Square.

Icelin said: "Where is Axaloe?"

Crust said: "Yes. We can hold him now as an accessory before or after."

Wingless said: "He must be upstairs. There's a small laboratory and his bedroom up there. I haven't seen him. It was Mary who opened the door to me." He made a queer stifled sound which may have been a laugh, and said hoarsely: "Imagine my embarrassment."

Maybe it was a sudden draught in the room that brought to the two men's nostrils a caress of Jane the Ripper's familiar perfume. And at the same time they heard the Duchess's cool clear voice, and her wide grey eyes for a moment rested on the men outside with a very level graciousness.

"Victor," she said, "won't your friends come in for a moment from the hot sun outside?"

In the dumbfounded silence that followed Wingless shifted his big limbs a little to one side so that the two men could not see within the room. His ruddy face was blotched with grey and the bruise on his jaw where Axaloe had hit him showed red and angry. Stooping forward he addressed his two friends in a low voice, but his pale eyes looked over their heads as though his mind was not on what he said.

"I can't presume to give a man in your position any advice, Icelin. But I can presume to suggest that you might never have got on to this man Axaloe but for the hint I gave you. At the moment I don't know whether I am standing on my head or my heels. But I do know, Crust, that we should make no move here until we have found out definitely if the Duchess of Dove is *at this moment still at Dr. Lapwing's nursing-home or not*. I can't tell you what I mean, since she is here. All I can tell you is to find out. There is no telephone here. You can trust me to take care of myself, and if Axaloe turns up rough I shall have the gardening implement you gave me. I suggest that you find a telephone and ring up the nursing-home in London. I shall stay here."

Now Crust did not know what to think, but his chief seemed to agree with the suggested plan. Icelin said later that he would have agreed with anything which would take him away from that damned house if only for a few minutes. The two men were walking down the garden path to the gate when Crust, without a word to Icelin, suddenly turned and strode back to the window where Wingless still stood.

"Sir," said Crust, in the loud voice of a man who wishes to be overheard, "I forgot to ask you something. Now do you identify, and will you so swear before God, the woman in the room behind you as the Duchess of Dove?"

"Before God," said Wingless, looking very intently down at Crust as though each word he spoke must be separately noted, "I do so identify this woman as the Duchess of Dove and from my experience and knowledge of her I do swear that in figure and person and voice and in all outward forms that are visible and audible this woman is the Duchess of Dove."

Crust, rejoining his chief by the gate, shook his head glumly.

"Sir," said he, "this is a rum business, and no mistake. Did you notice he distinctly said 'in all outward forms that are visible and audible'?"

"As God's above," said Icelin, "I wouldn't stay alone in a room with that inhuman woman for all the money in the world."

"Nor me," said Crust. "I hold Colonel Wingless, sir, to be the most courageous man I ever met or heard of."

CHAPTER FOURTEEN

But Colonel Wingless would not have agreed with his old friend Crust. When Mary Dove had first opened the door to him and greeted him in her dear familiar voice, he had been too stupefied by distress to think. Fear was to come later. Was the pursuit of the murderess known as Jane the Ripper at an end? Did she stand there now gazing at him with the gentle grey eyes of dear Mary?

"I had no idea," he said stupidly, "you were here, Mary."

"Dear Victor, I came this morning latish. I was so sorry to overhear your disagreement with Xanthis when you first called. He is such a nice man really that I am sure you will presently like him as much as I have grown to during the last few months."

"I thought I knew all your secrets, Mary. Why did you never tell me of your friendship with this man?"

They were now in the parlour, where the light was very restful after the glare outside. They stood near a round table piled high with heavy books from which the musty odour of ancient bindings rose to his nostrils as a welcome friend in an atmosphere which, he began to feel now, was outside normal experience.

And he was afraid. Standing a yard or so away from her familiar person, he stared intently into her face. Then, with an offensive particularity he would never have permitted himself with Mary in any other situation, he traced with his eyes the lines of her round breasts and of her slender feminine body beneath the white gown that she was wearing. When his eyes came back to her eyes he saw that she was smiling at him with a half-smile so mocking that his courage returned to him in a rush of anger at the change that had taken place in Mary Dove.

"Why," she said, "what a look from an old friend! Does my figure please you, Victor?"

He stretched out his right hand and caught a handful of her curly hair by the roots and held it tight enough to hurt. He wanted to know if this woman was not a figure made in Mary's image, if her face was not a lovely mask, if her hair was not a wig. But what happened to him was so unexpected that he could not at first realise what was happening. Her body yielded to him with a soft submissiveness that seemed to burn her tight round breasts into his chest, her parted lips were raised to his with an invitation which her sharp white teeth seemed to bite lecherously into his male consciousness. It was Mary's hair, Mary's fragrance, Mary's body. And it was very greedy, like a whore. She pressed her limbs to his, and her parted legs embraced his thigh with so urgent a fever of burning softness that her face suddenly flushed and her eyes half closed in a frenzy of anticipated pleasure. No wonder, he thought grimly, this woman had been described by coffee-stall keepers and the like as a "hot number." She was hotter than hell.

"I've always," she whispered, "wanted you, Victor."

He let her go, so that she almost fell, and he stood for an instant with closed eyes trying to find a power of reasoning within himself. For her lustfulness had sent an arrow into him so barbed with poison that he wondered if he was not as wanton as she. Mary was like a sister to him, he had always regarded her as his sister. And yet her desire could awaken his desire. When he opened his eyes she stood before him with a mantling flush which was like a noisome caricature of Mary's modesty.

"That *was* naughty of me, wasn't it, Victor? But the idea of having you has always excited me so much that just touching you set me——"

"How," he asked harshly, "did you manage to leave the nursing-home?"

"Darling, don't let us talk about dull things now. I was just having tea when you came. Won't you have a cup?"

She sat down by a small lacquered table. He felt his strength quite drained from him by the realisation that Mary, the gentlest and the most chaste of all the women he had ever met, had always in reality been hungry and thirsty and greedy for men. He threw himself into an armchair away from her near the window, and it was then that he spoke the words overheard by Crust and Icelin outside.

After the conversation already reported had taken place between the three men and Wingless turned back into the room, he saw a smile playing on her delicate profile.

"You look quite sane, Mary, but of course you must be a madwoman. What can you find to smile about when you know that presently you and Axaloe, who I suppose is your lover, are to be arrested for a series of the most horrible crimes ever committed by a woman?"

Smiling Mary's gentle smile, she said: "Darling, there's your whisky-and-soda, a nice stiff one. You will feel better after it. Now don't be afraid it's poisoned, because I've got too much use for your vitality to risk anything like that."

He drank the stimulant avidly, put the glass down on the table, and was in the act of sitting down again when, conscious of the intensity of her gaze on him, he looked across at her.

"Victor," she said, in a voice at once so clear and so alien to his experience that for an instant he wondered if he were on another planet, "Victor, go and lie down on that sofa."

He could see nothing at all but her eyes, nothing in the whole world but two eyes. And then he could see two black bright points. He wanted to shut his eyes tight against them, but he was without any will at all. And he felt the coils of a snake around him. He saw the two black bright points of a snake's eyes reared above his head. He felt his hands caressing the rough sensuous coils. Then he found himself lying on his back on the sofa with her body pressed down on him and her pointed tongue darting in and out of his mouth. The surface of her tongue was very rough, rougher than a woman's. He would have cried out, but he could not. How long he lay there powerless he could not tell, nor if he returned her raging kisses or answered to the convulsions of her frenzied limbs which slit her eyes so that he could see no more than their upturned whites. Then something happened which helped him to regain himself. The woman's crazy movements had naturally disarranged both his and her garments, and suddenly, where her gown had slipped from her shoulder, his eye caught something that was salmon-pink in colour. This slight distraction helped to counter her hypnotic power, and with a movement more brutal than he had ever thought it possible for him to make he threw her from him to the floor and got up. She lay where she had fallen digging her teeth into the backs of her own hands in a frenzy beyond all control and screaming: "How dare you? How dare you—just when I was going to——"

He took her from the floor by the slender nape of her neck. In the act of bending down he seemed to descend the steps of hell. With his open right hand he hit her as hard as he could on the side of her face. Then he let her fall to the floor again. She clung to his legs, arching her body upwards, and he kicked her away. She began whispering obscenities which were the more horrible because they were meant as endearments, and he hit her across the mouth with the back of his hand. She smiled at him with adoring eyes and pointed to a whip which stood in a corner.

He dared not leave her alone for fear she might escape, or he would have searched the house for Xanthis Axaloe. But he knew he would not find him. What did he know? Only that in this trim little house the laws that govern mankind had been degraded into another service than God's.

Stooping again, he turned her body and tore open her white gown and saw that beneath it her only covering was the salmon-pink bathing-costume which had so surprised him and Icelin on the masculine figure of Xanthis Axaloe. She twisted snakily in his grasp and buried her teeth in the back of his neck so that he felt the blood gush out. He rammed backwards with his elbow and she sighed as though with pleasure. At last, gasping with pain and disgust, he freed himself. She stood up, swaying, smiling, and her pointed rough tongue languished with delight between her red-flecked lips.

Wingless said: "You are not Mary Dove."

Her grey eyes were wide open and radiant and delighted. But he dared not meet them, concentrating as hard as he could on the lovely lips so fearfully disfigured.

She said: "Of course I'm not, you child."

"You are Xanthis Axaloe."

"Now," she said, "you are just being silly. You saw him in that nice bathing-costume and you felt enough of me when I was in your arms to know that we couldn't reasonably be one and the same person."

He glanced towards the window, wondering where Icelin was. Dear God, he must have help.

"You are Xanthis Axaloe," he repeated. "I don't know how, but you are."

"La-de-da," she said, "so Pan and Ishtar have become one, have they? And Priapus and Venus? Well, maybe. The march of science, of course, is irresistible. But what kind of magic can it be, my love, that can change a man into a woman so desirous of love and so capable, as you will find out, of fulfilling her desire?"

Terrified as a child in a dark room, he set his teeth and tried to reason himself back to sanity. What would happen to him alone with this woman if he cracked under the strain and fell quite into her power? He thought of the ripped and mutilated corpses which had marked Jane the Ripper's amorous adventures in London. And that was the fulfilment of her desire.

He had turned sideways to her, not to look at her, when suddenly he felt her moving towards him. A wave of panic which he made no attempt to control impelled him across the room to the window, as far away from her as he could get. Trembling, he sat on the sill and took out Crust's automatic and held it on his knees. Then, emboldened by the distance between them, he dared to look at her. She was smiling at him with a queer tolerant smile which somehow struck him as a more fearful thing even than all her amorousness. He could not tell why this was so until he realised that he sometimes would smile just that way at a dog he must punish for misbehaviour.

"Now," she said very gently, "the half of my desire is over."

He managed to grin, and felt a little the better for it.

"I hope," he said, "I can rely on that. What I simply cannot make out is: why the bathing-costume? First on Axaloe and then on you. And why the same bathing-costume?"

"My love," she said, "because it's so convenient. Of course it's very tight for Xanthis but it really looks very nice on me. Would you like to see it, darling?"

"I promise you," said Wingless, "that if you say 'darling' just once again I shall drill a hole in you with this gun."

She laughed Mary's dear laugh so naturally that he, who had fancied he was cured of the delusion that she really was Mary, felt himself withering with horror again.

"You *are* a silly boy," she said. "So you want to kill all the evil in the world, do you? And with a gun? It's really surprising what great faith men put in guns. My child, there is very much less evil in pagan ecstasy than in the filthy ingenuity that goes to the making of one toy revolver."

He said: "I know you are a murderess. I know you are a madwoman. But *who* are you?"

Then she cried out in a loud voice different from Mary's or from any other voice he had ever heard: "This is better than the old way. There is more delight. Oh, there is much more."

He said: "What was the old way? Who are you?" Then he heard her moving and he looked up and was lost. The two black bright points were glittering in his consciousness. He could not lift the automatic.

She cried out: "I am nameless."

Her face was so bright that his eyelids seemed to burn. But he could not close them.

She cried out: "I am nameless. I am soulless. I am eternal."

There was a narrow knife in her hand, and her fingers caressed the slender blade. He could not move.

"You can't imagine," she said, in that voice of hers so strange to his ears that he wondered if she was not speaking a forgotten language, "you can't imagine what a fool I once was. Do you know that I used to bore myself sitting for years upon years within stone images while people worshipped me and the priests sacrificed youths and maidens by opening their throats and cutting out their hearts. It may have been fun for the priests, but you can imagine I was bored to death."

He forced himself to say: "You are no more than an evil madman who has found some godless means of changing his body."

"It is more polite, my love, to speak in symbols. Let us say that I am sin incarnate and sin triumphant. Let us say that I was born before the beginning and shall outlive the end. Let us say that the serpent is the father and mother of all the worms that men become. I don't in the least mind you thinking that I am no more than a scientist with evil powers. After all, research should always be encouraged. But you will change your mind, my love, in the delicious agonies before your death."

A voice from the garden behind him said something. There was a tremble in Icelin's voice. Wingless could not hear what he said, could not answer. He prayed to God to give Icelin the courage to come in and distract the two bright black points of the monster's eyes from him. Then Icelin came in.

Wingless shouted: "Don't look at her, man."

CHAPTER FIFTEEN

SHE was so calm and so self-possessed that Icelin, pale though he himself was, could not but look at his friend with surprise. Wingless, his shirt sticking to him with sweat, strove to attain even a small degree of composure. At Icelin's entrance the woman seemed instantly to dwindle to her ordinary stature. And her unbearable radiance was put out like a light, so that now it was none other than Mary Dove who sat so calmly on a tapestried footstool by the empty fireplace. He realised, having seen that face transfigured, that he could never again think of the real Mary as anything but merely pretty. The woman, quite undisturbed by a second man's presence, sat playing idly with the narrow shining knife. Icelin's eyes goggled at it.

Wingless said: "You came just in time, Icelin. Take no notice of her now. I think maybe we've got her at last."

Icelin said: "The Duchess is in the nursing-home. I spoke to the doctor himself. She could not have moved if she had wanted to, because she is dying."

"Of course," Mary's voice said idly from the woman's mouth.

Icelin, wetting his lips, said: "The doctor doesn't know why. She seems to be dying of nothing more than weakness. And fear. She lies with her eyes closed because she says that when they are open she sees nothing but two black bright points and she says that she is quite certain there is a snake in the room."

Wingless said: "Maybe we shall deal with that snake presently. What about the girl?"

"Monica Snee has confessed to helping the man Axaloe. He found means of meeting her after his first call at Grosvenor Square, and she became his mistress. At first she thought he was nothing more than an anarchist. Then she says she found he was some kind of a god or what-not. She dithered a good deal about the ecstasy of the circle. And she's got snakes on the brain, too. She said he picked on the Duchess because sin triumphant must wear the body of the most chaste. She concealed him in the house several times, and on two occasions borrowed the Duchess's clothes for him."

"I returned them," said the woman gently, "and without so much as a spot of blood on them, either. Though I must say that that attractive young man I met on the Tottenham Court Road was——"

Wingless said: "What about Crust?"

"There's the devil to pay. A wrecking mob has got out of

hand, and the county police have all they can do to keep them from burning every big house in the neighbourhood. And they are all screaming for the Duchess's head on a plate."

Wingless said: "Nothing would please us more than to let them have it, but they'd never believe it wasn't the real Duchess."

"But you'll have to give it to them, won't you?" the woman asked softly. "Or would you like to let me go upstairs to my laboratory for five minutes?"

Then she looked for the first time directly at Icelin, who still stood with his back to the closed door.

Wingless said: "Don't look at her, you fool. She'll put one of us against the other before we know it. Icelin, I'll have a talk with Crust's sister-in-law if ever we get out of this house alive. This chap Axaloe seems to have discovered that there are not only fairies at the bottom of the garden but that he can change himself into one." He turned to the woman, keeping his eyes low. "Is it your idea that I can't kill you?"

"When you do, my love, you will kill yourself."

Wingless said: "I'll take that risk. I have an idea that Mary will live if she no longer feels that there is a snake in her room."

"In her bed," said the woman. "That's why she is dying of horror."

Wingless said: "I shall kill you because I'd rather die than live with the thought that such a thing as you can walk in the sunlight."

"Silly!" smiled the woman. "I am soulless. I am not made by God. How can you kill me? I always come back, for I am that which was born before the beginning and shall outlive the end."

And she was looking hungrily at Icelin.

Wingless said: "You had better tie a handkerchief round

your eyes, Icelin. Hell's like an ice-box to our girl friend when she starts one of her mild flirtations. Now when I make a grab at her, do as you are told. This is an execution, and we'll have time to ask forgiveness later."

Icelin, trying in vain to blink his eyes away from the woman, said sharply; "We can't, man. It's murder, whatever she is. And if you try it, I shall stop you. A fine stink it would make when it was known that Scotland Yard had helped to murder a criminal."

Wingless said: "I am going to kill this thing in the shape of a woman and you are not going to stop me."

The woman's slender gracious figure rose from the stool. With an idle gesture she laid the knife on the table, and then she turned to Wingless. She stretched out her long white arms.

Icelin said: "O God, look at her!"

Wingless knew what effect the woman's transfigured unearthly beauty was making on his friend. Then he felt her evil radiance scorching him, and he fought very powerfully with the fear and disgust that stopped him from touching her. Suddenly Icelin began yelling like a madman and as in a dream Wingless saw him fighting frantically with the monster. But Wingless was in the grip of a sweet and overpowering languor and even when Icelin finally managed to drag the vampire's teeth from his throat it seemed to him a very distasteful thing that he must move. Only Icelin's sobs aroused him. The woman, now utterly inhuman in the climax of her fearful enjoyment, sat astride Icelin's body on the floor with her knees pressed ecstatically into his sides, crooning an incantation in an unknown tongue which was like a rushing wind through trees. Wingless, tying his handkerchief round his torn throat, gripped her round her slender middle. He could overcome his repulsion only by closing his eyes, and he found himself thinking of the time when as a small boy he had hurled himself on a bigger boy with his eyes tight shut because he was afraid. Icelin managed to wriggle away from beneath the thing, but it was all the two powerful men could do to hold her down. Her snake-like convulsions between their hands were very horrible to them and continued even when Icelin had tied her feet together.

Then they carried her to the divan against the far wall. Neither man dared look at her lovely face, and both felt ashamed as they tied her slender wrists together behind her back. In this room these men had seen the traditional walls of human life broken down, yet they could not free themselves from the trivial conventions which men and women have built for their self-protection.

Wingless took out his automatic. The woman was smiling so gentle a smile that Icelin could not bear to look and turned away. Her grey eyes looked up with passionate delight at the fair man towering above her. He pressed the muzzle of the automatic down into the flesh below her breast-bones and, his eyes closed, pulled the trigger twice. In the terrible silence that followed the crash he could hear Icelin's sobbing breath. The smell of smoke and burning cloth enveloped him. Very afraid of looking down at what he had done, he stood frozen. Then Icelin gave a fearful scream and Wingless, forcing himself to open his eyes, saw Axaloe's stern dark features forming mistily over the woman's fair face. Axaloe's deep icy eyes were smiling with sardonic amusement.

"You fool," he said. "I am eternal. But you shall die."

Then such a rage possessed Wingless that nothing Icelin could say or do could stop his passion to destroy. Icelin kept on shouting: "Let him change, man. We must arrest him and find out how. . . ."

His great hands encircling Axaloe's throat, Wingless

pressed down for what seemed to him an eternity. Axaloe, opening his mouth wide in his dying agony, spoke a sentence in a language that sounded like a rushing wind. Wingless, at last unloosening his hands, turned blindly away and lurched to the door.

He said: "We've got to burn this house and all that's in it. I'll get some petrol from the car."

Icelin did not answer. His face crumbling with horror, he pointed towards Axaloe's body, and at the same time Wingless felt himself submerged in a stench so vile that no man's senses could bear it. Without glancing round he dashed out of the house, Icelin at his heels. They ran on, out of the garden and down the lane, until they had left the stench of corruption behind them.

"The monkey-house at the Zoo," Icelin gasped, "multipled ten thousand times."

Wingless had stopped dead and was looking at his hands, first at their palms and then turning them over.

He said: "I didn't turn round. What was it?"

Icelin said: "It wasn't a body."

"What was it?"

Icelin started walking on, almost running. Wingless remained where he was, still looking at his hands. Then he raised them to his nostrils. Icelin, setting his teeth, came back.

"Come on, man. Let's get it over. Though I wonder if we can face that stench again."

Wingless said: "What was it, Icelin? I didn't look round. What did you see?"

"I can't tell you. I want never to think of it again. I'll go mad if I do." Then Icelin said: "There wasn't a body. There was that white dress floating in something greyish that slopped over on to the floor. . . ."

The corners of Wingless's mouth twitched.

"O Christ," he whispered, "was that what I touched?"

Icelin said: "Let's forget it, man. Let's try."

They walked on to the car, and Wingless got out a spare tin of petrol. Icelin looked curiously at his friend's grey face. Wingless unstopped a tin and very carefully poured some of the petrol over first one hand and then the other.

Icelin said: "What's that for?"

Wingless gave him the tin, then rubbed his moist hands hard together for several seconds. Then he raised them to his nostrils again, and sniffed.

Icelin said: "What the hell's the matter?"

Wingless gave him a long searching look. His eyes were cold, like a stranger's.

"You don't smell anything, Icelin?"

"Here? Thank God, no. Only petrol."

Wingless nodded thoughtfully, and dug his hands deep into his pockets as though he wanted them out of sight. Icelin, holding the tin carefully, turned towards the house.

"We'll have to face it again, Wingless, beastly though it is. We have to burn that house and the thing in it. The police will report that Jane the Ripper burned herself to death, and the public will damn well have to believe it or not as they like."

Wingless said: "You'll have to do it alone. I am not coming. I'm through. You can take the car when you've finished."

Icelin stared at him.

"What are you going to do, Wingless?"

"I don't know. Leave me alone."

He turned and walked down the lane towards Leatherhead. For a long time Icelin stared after the tall figure of his friend. Wingless walked very clumsily with his hands deep in his pockets. And it was many weeks before Icelin, or any friend of his, saw Colonel Wingless again. But Icelin's servant, who was a friend of the Colonel's servant, occasionally gave him reports.

It appeared that Wingless was obsessed with the idea that his hands exuded an unbearable stench of corruption. It was a certainty, not an idea. This odour made his body, and particularly his hands, unbearable to him. No one could smell this but himself, but he was positive that his servants and the doctors whom he consulted said this only out of kindness. He sat indoors all day long with his hands wrapped in perfumed cloths. But this did no good, and he steamed the skin from his hands. He described this smell which pursued him from his own person day and night as being like that of the monkey-house at the Zoo multiplied ten thousand times. He would not see even Mary Dove who, her health almost regained, lived in even greater seclusion than before and was venerated by all gentlefolk for the shameful misfortunes that had so nearly destroyed her.

Some five months later Colonel Wingless blew his brains out. He left no message of any kind. His many friends must always mourn the pitiful end of a loyal friend, a fearless rider to hounds, and a very gallant gentleman.

THE END

NEW AND FORTHCOMING TITLES FROM VALANCOURT BOOKS

R. C. Ashby (Ruby Ferguson)	He Arrived at Dusk
Frank Baker	The Birds
Walter Baxter	Look Down in Mercy
Charles Beaumont	The Hunger and Other Stories
David Benedictus	The Fourth of June
Paul Binding	Harmonica's Bridegroom
John Blackburn	A Scent of New-Mown Hay
	Broken Boy
	Blue Octavo
	The Flame and the Wind
	Nothing But the Night
	Bury Him Darkly
	The Household Traitors
	Our Lady of Pain
	The Face of the Lion
	The Cyclops Goblet
	A Beastly Business
Thomas Blackburn	The Feast of the Wolf
John Braine	Room at the Top
	The Vodi
Basil Copper	The Great White Space
	Necropolis
Hunter Davies	Body Charge
Jennifer Dawson	The Ha-Ha
Barry England	Figures in a Landscape
Ronald Fraser	Flower Phantoms
Stephen Gilbert	The Landslide
	Bombardier
	Monkeyface
	The Burnaby Experiments
	Ratman's Notebooks
Martyn Goff	The Plaster Fabric
	The Youngest Director
	Indecent Assault
Stephen Gregory	The Cormorant
Thomas Hinde	Mr. Nicholas
	The Day the Call Came
Claude Houghton	I Am Jonathan Scrivener
	This Was Ivor Trent

Gerald Kersh	Nightshade and Damnations
	Fowlers End
	Night and the City
	On an Odd Note
Francis King	To the Dark Tower
	Never Again
	An Air That Kills
	The Dividing Stream
	The Dark Glasses
	The Man on the Rock
C.H.B. Kitchin	Ten Pollitt Place
	The Book of Life
Hilda Lewis	The Witch and the Priest
Kenneth Martin	Aubade
	Waiting for the Sky to Fall
Michael McDowell	The Amulet
Michael Nelson	Knock or Ring
	A Room in Chelsea Square
Beverley Nichols	Crazy Pavements
Oliver Onions	The Hand of Kornelius Voyt
Dennis Parry	Sea of Glass
Robert Phelps	Heroes and Orators
J.B. Priestley	Benighted
	The Other Place
	The Magicians
Peter Prince	Play Things
Forrest Reid	The Garden God
	Following Darkness
	At the Door of the Gate
	The Spring Song
	Brian Westby
	The Tom Barber Trilogy
	Denis Bracknel
David Storey	Radcliffe
	Pasmore
	Saville
Russell Thorndike	The Slype
	The Master of the Macabre
John Trevena	Furze the Cruel
	Sleeping Waters
John Wain	Hurry on Down
	The Smaller Sky

Hugh Walpole	The Killer and the Slain
Keith Waterhouse	There is a Happy Land
	Billy Liar
Colin Wilson	Ritual in the Dark
	Man Without a Shadow
	The World of Violence
	The Philosopher's Stone
	The God of the Labyrinth

Selected Eighteenth and Nineteenth Century Classics

Anonymous	Teleny
	The Sins of the Cities of the Plain
Grant Allen	Miss Cayley's Adventures
Joanna Baillie	Six Gothic Dramas
Eaton Stannard Barrett	The Heroine
William Beckford	Azemia
Mary Elizabeth Braddon	Thou Art the Man
John Buchan	Sir Quixote of the Moors
Hall Caine	The Manxman
Marie Corelli	The Sorrows of Satan
	Ziska
Baron Corvo	Stories Toto Told Me
	Hubert's Arthur
Gabriele D'Annunzio	The Intruder (L'innocente)
Arthur Conan Doyle	Round the Red Lamp
	The Parasite
Baron de la Motte Fouqué	The Magic Ring
H. Rider Haggard	Nada the Lily
Sheridan Le Fanu	Carmilla
M. G. Lewis	The Monk
Edward Bulwer Lytton	Eugene Aram
Florence Marryat	The Blood of the Vampire
Richard Marsh	The Beetle
	The Goddess: A Demon
Bertram Mitford	Renshaw Fanning's Quest
John Moore	Zeluco
Ouida	Under Two Flags
Walter Pater	Marius the Epicurean
Bram Stoker	The Lady of the Shroud
	The Mystery of the Sea

Lightning Source UK Ltd.
Milton Keynes UK
UKOW051454170713

213952UK00002B/14/P